TRAPPED!

"Quick! Get down here!" a voice whispered from the darkness.

Regina didn't waste any time. She slid through the door and Stevie followed right after her.

It wasn't completely dark. A dim light shone from a single bulb in the middle of the basement ceiling. Peter, Liza, Ann, and Gordon were all huddled under it.

Peter had a silencing finger at his lips. Stevie couldn't imagine why, but the look of terror on Gordon's face told her that there was a reason.

"Someone's upstairs," Ann whispered, barely audible.

Stevie sat down on the box next to Liza and listened. Someone *was* upstairs. They could hear footsteps on the front steps leading up to the house's main entrance on the parlor floor. There was the click of a key turning in the lock. . . .

the SADDLE CLUB

HARD HAT

BONNIE BRYANT

A SKYLARK BOOK
NEW YORK • TORONTO • LONDON • SYDNEY • AUCKLAND

Special thanks to Sir "B" Farms and Laura Roper

RL 3.6, ages 008–012

HARD HAT
A Bantam Skylark Book / March 2001

ISBN 0-553-48739-6

Visit us on the Web! www.randomhouse.com/kids

**Educators and librarians, for a variety of teaching tools, visit us at
www.randomhouse.com/teachers**

Published simultaneously in the United States and Canada

Bantam Skylark is an imprint of Random House Children's Books, a division of
Random House, Inc. SKYLARK BOOK and colophon and BANTAM
BOOKS and colophon are registered trademarks of Random House, Inc.
Bantam Books, 1540 Broadway, New York, New York 10036.

PRINTED IN THE UNITED STATES OF AMERICA

OPM   10 9 8 7 6 5 4 3 2 1

For my cousins, Peter and Michael—

with love,

Bonnie

"HEY, GUYS! We've got to hurry up!" Stevie Lake said, glancing at her watch. She was walking with her two best friends, Lisa Atwood and Carole Hanson, toward their favorite place in the world to do their favorite thing: to Pine Hollow Stables to ride horses.

"What time is it?" Carole asked, picking up her pace.

"It's already ten minutes to eight!" Stevie said, walking even faster.

That made Lisa walk faster still. If there was one thing Max Regnery hated, it was lateness from his students. In fact, he hated it so much, he referred to it as

1

tardiness, which meant the same thing as being late but sounded much more serious.

"How did it get to be sooo—" Lisa asked, trying to look at her own watch, which was hard to do at the pace she was walking.

She stopped. Her watch said 7:30. "Stevie time," she announced. Carole stopped, too. The two girls began laughing.

"I told you you'd get into trouble setting your watch twenty minutes fast," Lisa said.

"Well, I wasn't going to be late," Stevie said sheepishly. The girls continued their walk at a normal pace.

"I don't mind *you* getting into trouble," Carole said. "It's when you get *us* into trouble along with you that bothers me."

"So what else is new?" Lisa asked. The girls laughed again. Reluctantly, Stevie reset her watch to the correct time. They were about five minutes from the stable, and that would give them plenty of time to check on their horses before Max called their Pony Club meeting to order at 8:00 A.M. sharp.

Carole breathed in the clean, fresh air, almost certain she could detect the sweet smell of horses and fresh hay from where she stood. Although the three girls could hardly have been more different from one another, their bond of friendship was sealed by a common love of horses. In fact, they loved horses so much that soon after they'd first met, they had formed their own club: The Saddle Club. It had only two rules, and the first one was easy: All members had to be horse-crazy. That was a test all three of them passed with flying colors. The other rule was more difficult, though they were generally willing to follow it: Members had to be willing to help each other out, no matter what. That was a rule that had gotten them into trouble almost as many times as it had been exercised to get them out of it.

As they walked along the country lane that led to Pine Hollow, Lisa glanced at Stevie and smiled, thinking about her watch. It was typical of her to try to fix a problem (chronic lateness) and thus create another (panic). Stevie was more creative about ways to get into trouble than anybody else Lisa had ever known. When you asked Stevie how her school day was, the answer was invariably peppered with explanations about what she'd had to say to Miss Fenton—her school's headmistress—when she'd been sent to her office *that* day.

Stevie wasn't bad. She wasn't even naughty or a troublemaker. She thought of herself as being creative—in ways teachers were inclined to think unnecessary. Lisa remembered hearing about the time Stevie had managed to get food coloring into the vat of mashed potatoes. Green potatoes on St. Patrick's Day had seemed like a great idea to Stevie. Somehow, the cafeteria workers at Fenton Hall had not been amused, just as her biology teacher hadn't been impressed by Stevie's claim that one of her brothers had substituted a disappearing ink pen for the one that Stevie had thought she was using for her homework, now a sheaf of blank pages.

Even though Stevie was a practical joker, she had a big heart. Nobody came to other people's rescue faster than Stevie did, and nobody cared more about others. It was as if her own troubles made her understand how much other people could need her. But if someone annoyed her, Stevie's hot temper could flare.

Carole and Lisa loved her with all their hearts. Sometimes Lisa thought it was because Stevie was everything she could never be. For all of Stevie's flamboyance and unpredictability, Lisa was calm, organized, logical, and coolheaded. Lisa was a straight-A student, and she never missed homework deadlines.

Her clothes were always clean and neatly pressed, her hair always smooth and combed.

Lisa's older brother, Peter, didn't live at home anymore, so Lisa felt like an only child. Lisa often wondered what it was like for Stevie to live with three brothers. Chad was older, Alex was Stevie's twin, and Michael was the youngest. Sometimes it seemed like Stevie was at war with all three of them. Lisa's mother had wanted the best for her daughter and saw to it that Lisa had all the opportunities she and Lisa's father could reasonably give her. Her mother's idea of giving Lisa the best was to have Lisa take lessons in everything she considered proper for a young girl. Lisa had studied dance, violin, piano, voice, ballet, painting, even needlepoint. But all those activities lost their appeal the day Mrs. Atwood had decided Lisa should learn a little bit about horses—as every young lady should. Lisa didn't want to learn a little bit about horses. She'd found that after her first lessons, she'd wanted to learn everything in the world there was to know about the horses!

Carole and Stevie had been there to help her learn, and Carole especially was the perfect person for that. Of the three horse-crazy girls, there was no doubt that

Carole was the horse-craziest. From the time she was four, she'd known that all she ever wanted to do in her life was to work with horses. She knew she had a lot of options. She could ride, train, breed, race, compete, care for, or heal them. Or she could do all of those. She hadn't decided which career with horses would be just right for her, but she knew it would be one of them.

As the threesome walked up Pine Hollow's driveway, the whole place seemed in disarray. There was more confusion than usual, and the first hint of it was that Max was dashing across the driveway, knees bent, arms extended, trying to catch his daughter, a rambunctious toddler named Maxi, short for Maxine.

"Stop that child!" he declared in time for Lisa to pick up the little girl. Maxi had a delighted grin on her face. She clearly thought this was a game and she'd won. Lisa gave her a little hug before handing her back to her father.

"Meeting starts in ten minutes sharp!" Max announced as if he were ready for it to begin, which he obviously wasn't.

"Right," Carole said, snapping him a smart salute.

"Has anyone seen Red?" Max asked. Red was Pine Hollow's head stable hand.

"No, we just got here," Stevie reminded him.

"Right, well, somebody's going to have to look after Maxi."

"Don't you mean *chase* after Maxi?" Lisa suggested.

"That, too," Max said. He left, apparently in search of a temporary baby-sitter.

Twenty minutes later Max called the meeting to order. Horse Wise, which was the Pine Hollow chapter of the U.S. Pony Clubs, met every Saturday morning. Max usually alternated weeks of mounted and unmounted meetings, meaning that one week their meeting would be on horseback, working on riding skills, and the next week they'd meet in Max's office and have a presentation or discussion of stable management, veterinary care, shoeing, or some other important aspect of horse care and ownership. Today's discussion was on the general subject of safety.

Max stood in front of the group, holding Maxi on his left hip.

"All right, then," Max said, frowning at the clock on the back wall. "Who can tell me some of the things we have here to protect riders?"

"Helmets," said Joe. Max nodded. Riding helmets were required of all riders whenever they were on horseback.

"The mounting block," said May, reminding every-one that a secure beginning to a ride was always a good idea.

"The good-luck horseshoe," said Jasmine. Everyone nodded. One of Pine Hollow's traditions was a horse-shoe nailed over the door that every rider touched be-fore beginning a ride. Some people claimed it had magical powers because no rider had ever been seri-ously hurt at Pine Hollow. Most riders recognized that it was more a matter of reminding all riders that the sport could be dangerous and they needed to take pre-cautions. Whatever the reasons, it seemed to work.

Maxi wriggled, trying to loosen Max's grasp. She pounded her father on top of his head and wriggled some more. Absentmindedly, he put her down.

"Deborah is away today," he said, explaining the obvious. Deborah, Max's wife, was an investigative re-porter for a major Washington newspaper. "And she's working on a story, so even when she's home, like she will be tomorrow, she'll be too busy to look after Maxi for a couple of days."

Lisa grabbed for the fleeing child. Max nodded with pleasure when he saw that Maxi was secure—for a few minutes at least. Clearly he was a little befuddled

by his joint responsibilities as father and riding in-
structor.

Lisa plopped Maxi down on her lap and handed the
girl a pencil and some paper to scribble on. There was
a moment of quiet, and Max continued the meeting.

"And safety precautions for the horses?" he asked.
There were lots of answers, including locks on their
stable doors, bandages for their legs when they traveled, careful feeding, shoeing, and preventive vet care.

Maxi dropped the pencil and paper, got up from
Lisa's lap, and trundled over to look at the shiny gold
chain around Veronica diAngelo's neck. She reached
for it.

"Eeew!" said Veronica, recoiling from the little girl's
moist grasp and wrinkling her nose.

Max sighed. "Needs a change?" he asked. Veronica
nodded distastefully.

"I'll do it," Lisa volunteered. Max thanked her and
handed her a diaper bag. Lisa picked up Maxi and
took her into the bathroom. She loved Maxi, as did
her friends. In fact, they'd been there when she'd been
born, looking after Deborah all the way through her
labor until the newest generation of Regnerys arrived.

A few minutes later Lisa returned to the Horse

Wise meeting and settled down, once again trying to contain the little girl she'd taken as her charge. It didn't work. Maxi went from lap to lap, interrupting the meeting repeatedly. Nobody really minded, except perhaps Veronica, but nobody cared what Veronica thought anyway.

Veronica diAngelo was The Saddle Club's least favorite rider. She was the daughter of one of Willow Creek's wealthiest citizens, and she never let anyone forget it. She considered herself better than everyone, and the result was that she wasn't as good as anyone. She hated doing her own chores, and her only spark of creativity was in finding ways to get other people to do her jobs. This was not a popular attitude at a stable built on cooperation and shared work.

Once their meeting was over, the riders prepared for riding class. Today they were going to work on jumping techniques and, as a sideline, baby-sitting. The riders took turns looking after Maxi, who had been fitted with a riding helmet, just to be on the safe side.

It turned out that Maxi's hard hat was a good idea. Although she managed to stay out of the way of the horses, Maxi wasn't awfully secure on her feet, and she fell down several times. Stevie was picking her up for the third time and giving her bumped knee a kiss when Deborah arrived. Maxi ran to her mother, arms open for a big hug, which Deborah seemed more than happy to give. She set down her computer and the bagful of notes she was carrying in order to embrace her daughter. A few seconds later the two of them joined the watchers at the rail of the jumping class.

Max was working with Katya, a very new rider, on basic skills. It wasn't that everybody couldn't benefit from review, but The Saddle Club had a thorough knowledge of the material, so they took the opportunity to chat with Deborah. Max was apparently so pleased not to have to worry about Maxi for a few minutes that he didn't even glare when they stepped aside to talk.

"Was she a nuisance?" Deborah asked.

"Just a little bit," Stevie said.

"No, she was mostly just fun to be with," Carole assured Deborah.

"And chase after," Stevie added.

"And hold," said Lisa.

"So, tell us about the story you're working on," Stevie said. "Max said it's really important."

Deborah smiled. "He would say that. Well, it's pretty important, anyway. It's about corruption."

Deborah wasn't just any reporter: She was an investigative reporter, which meant she would look for stories that required a lot of background and research to put together, and she'd often uncover crimes and misdeeds. It was sometimes dangerous, but it was always interesting.

"It's about the construction industry here. See, there's so much building going on that some of the people can get away with overcharging people for their work. And when they do, I've found cases where they then proceed to do shoddy work and pocket the difference. Some of these guys are getting away with murder."

"Murder?" Stevie echoed.

"Well, not really murder. But lots and lots of money. And in some cases they use a portion of that money to pay off building inspectors to say a building is safe when in fact it might not be."

"That's terrible!" Carole said.

"Somebody ought to do something!" said Lisa.

"I am," Deborah assured them. "I mean, I will—right after I give Maxi some lunch!"

"We can help," said Lisa.

"No, you've got your class now."

"I don't mean now," Lisa said. "I mean we can help with Maxi while you're working on the research for your story. Max has to teach classes, but when we're not in the classes we can certainly baby-sit. Right, girls?" She looked at Carole and Stevie.

Sometimes, when The Saddle Club wasn't busy helping one another out, they had what they'd come to think of as Saddle Club projects. They usually decided together that they were going to pitch in to do something. This time, it seemed Lisa was volunteering their services. On the other hand, it was perfectly clear to all of them that Max and Deborah needed their help and they were able to give it.

"I'll pay you," Deborah offered. "I mean, the usual baby-sitting rate."

That clinched it. All three girls nodded and smiled. Getting paid to do something they liked as much as chasing after Maxi was a very good deal.

AFTER CLASS THE girls hurried over to Stevie's house for their planned sleepover. When they had showered and changed their clothes, they met in the Lake kitchen for a snack. Lisa was full of ideas about ways to look after Maxi.

"We can switch off days. I'll take Monday. Carole you do Tuesday, Stevie Wednesday."

"Wouldn't it be more fun and easier if there were two of us at any one time?" Stevie asked.

13

"Okay by me," Lisa said. "Now, as to activities. We can read her books about ponies, and she likes to draw things."

"Scribble," Stevie corrected her.

"Well, yes, but don't you think Picasso started with scribbles?"

"I bet she'd like to play with clay," Carole suggested.

Fifteen minutes later the girls had a long list of activities for Maxi and a pretty good idea of when each of them would be caring for her. Stevie smiled, looking at Lisa. There were some real advantages to having a truly organized friend.

"Oh, Stevie! There you are!" Mrs. Lake hurried into the kitchen, an excited look on her face.

"Mrs. Lake, you should know by now that the best place to find Stevie is always in the kitchen," Carole teased.

"You're right about that," said Stevie's mother.

"What's up?" Stevie asked.

"We are!" she said. "I mean, you and I are going on a trip!"

"We are?"

"I've got to be in New York City next week on business and I've arranged to stay with my college friend Elisa Evans. You remember Mrs. Evans, don't you?"

Stevie didn't remember her, but she didn't think that mattered very much. She just nodded.

"Well, she lives in this big house on the Upper East Side and she's got a daughter almost exactly your age. In fact, Elisa and I were pregnant at the same time. I haven't met Regina—that's her daughter—but Elisa has told me a lot about her and I think the two of you are going to get along just fine. Actually . . . from what she said, I'm a little worried that you're going to get along too well. Apparently Regina is quite a prankster. That reminds me, I got a call from Miss Fenton's office . . ."

"You mean I'm going to New York with you?" Stevie asked, thinking it would be a good idea to skip the question about Miss Fenton's office.

"If you want to," said Mrs. Lake. "It should be a lot of fun. I mean, museums, theaters, restaurants—you know how great that city is. And you'll get to meet Regina. Elisa and I are sure you're going to like each other. Want to come?"

Stevie looked at her friends. She felt bad about leaving after they'd just planned a whole Saddle Club project baby-sitting Maxi. *Hmmm. Maxi: mud pies, diapers, smeared spaghetti, splattered finger paint. New York: museums, subways, restaurants, new friends.*

Stevie scratched her head.

"Oh, stop it!" Lisa said.

"Stop what?" Stevie asked.

"Stop pretending there's anything to decide!" said Lisa. "Of course you're going to New York. The only problem is that Carole and I wish we could come, too!"

"Definitely," Carole agreed.

"You don't mind me leaving you with Maxi?" Stevie asked.

"Not a bit," Carole assured her. "All the more baby-sitting money for the two of us."

Stevie grinned. "You guys are the best," she said.

"It's decided, then," said Mrs. Lake. "We'll leave Monday morning."

2

"HEY, LOOK! IT'S the Empire State Building!" Carole announced, handing a postcard to Lisa.

The two of them were at Pine Hollow, looking after Maxi, when Mrs. Reg handed them their first postcard from Stevie.

"She's having fun," Lisa said, looking at the scribbled note.

"Of course she is. She's in New York. What does she say?"

"Hmmm. 'New York is great,' " she read. " 'But you already know that. We didn't go to the Empire State Building, but the picture was so N.Y. that I couldn't resist. Mom was right, Regina is my kind of girl. You'd

17

love her, too. The first thing we did when I got here was climb over the fence in her backyard. We got chased by a dog, but that's another story. The only thing missing in this wonderful place is you and Pine Hollow and horses and TD's and Max. Well, it's still a great place!'"

"Hmmph," Carole grunted. "She's completely forgotten that there are horses in New York."

"And we rode them," said Lisa.

"Right," Carole agreed. "That's where we met . . ."

"SKYE RANSOM," STEVIE said.

"You really met, like, the *real* Skye Ransom? Here?" Regina asked.

Stevie nodded. She was sitting in Regina's backyard with a group of Regina's friends from the neighborhood. The backyard and the neighborhood were like nothing else Stevie had ever seen. Almost the whole block was made up of houses, but not houses like they had in Willow Creek. These were taller, narrower, and closer together—in fact they were touching. Most of them were four stories tall, and they seemed to have only a front and back room on each story. Stevie had learned that they were called brownstones, after the brown sandstone that covered the exterior of most of them. Some were actually brick, but it didn't seem to matter. They were still called brownstones. And behind each one was a yard, carefully fenced and dividing a large open area in the center of the block.

None of the yards was very large, and except for the fact that they were pretty much the same size and shape, they were all unique. Most of them had some plants and grass, though a few were just concrete. Some had play things for children. Others had chairs and tables and barbecue grills. A few had trees to climb. Most of the fences were not very high, though they did provide some privacy for each of the gardens.

Best of all, as far as Stevie was concerned, almost all the fences could be climbed, and many of them were of wide brick that made them perfect for walking along, as long as you took extra care for balance. It had taken Stevie only about four minutes to fall in love with the place. Because the houses were big, most of them with four or more bedrooms, there were a lot of children of different ages. On the warm, sunny summer days, they all played together.

Stevie felt comfortable with Regina and her friends and quickly got the hang of going from garden to garden, playing at other kids' houses, with other kids' pets and other kids' games. She especially liked when other kids' parents handed out cookies and milk, totally unaware of the fact that they'd just gotten snacks two houses away! New York was great.

"Absolutely, we met Skye Ransom," Stevie said. "And the next time you see him ride a horse in a movie, you should know who taught him everything he knows about riding."

"You're kidding," said Ann, a girl who lived next door to the Evanses. "I read in a magazine that he's a good rider."

"He is *now*!" Stevie told her. And then she explained about how she and her friends had been riding in Central Park when they'd found Skye, who'd just been thrown from his horse. It was only because of their coaching that he was able to keep his riding ignorance a secret from the movie director and learn enough to succeed in his scenes on horseback.

"What a story!" said Liza, who lived across the way. Liza reminded Stevie of Lisa. She had a sweet girlish quality and a neat appearance that made her seem like she would never get dirty or wrinkled. She was also a little shy; but compared to Regina, anybody might appear shy.

"It's true. It really is," Stevie said.

"I'm sure," said Peter, Ann's older brother. Only he said it in a tone that meant he wasn't at all sure. "Anyway, who cares about Skye Ransom?"

"Professional jealousy?" Stevie asked, teasing.

"I plead the Fifth," said Peter. He was a nice guy. Stevie had liked him from the minute she met him. He and Ann had a little brother, Gordon, who reminded Stevie of her own little brother, Michael. Stevie's brother could be something of a nuisance on occasion, but she loved him dearly—even though she'd never dream of telling him that. Peter seemed to feel the same way about Gordon and didn't even mind the fact that Gordon always wanted to tag along with the older kids. Ann tolerated both of her brothers well—much better than Stevie did her own brothers. Ann was almost exactly the same age as Stevie and Regina. Peter was two years older and Gordon three years younger. The three of them were unmistakably siblings, each having straight dark brown hair, intense gray eyes, and mischievous smiles. One glance and Stevie had known they'd be people she liked.

Stevie had learned that Peter, Ann, and Gordon's father was a doctor whose office was in their house. Ann's bedroom was on the third floor—the same floor on the same side of the house as Regina's. It was possible, though not necessarily wise, to go from one girl's bedroom to the other via the fire escapes on each of the houses. "We have to hold on really tight," Regina explained. "And we never, ever, tell our mothers."

"Never," Ann agreed.

"Let's play," said Regina.

"Play what?" asked Liza.

"Hide-and-seek," Regina said. "Stevie and I will pair up for now since she doesn't know the place at all. And, um, Peter, you're It!"

Peter dutifully closed his eyes and began counting out loud. "One one thousand, two one thousand, three one thousand . . ."

"C'mon. We only have until one hundred," Regina said, grabbing Stevie's hand.

Quick as could be, the girls scaled the fence and dashed along the brick wall to the left of Regina's house. The others were scattering rapidly, too.

Stevie followed Regina, who led her along the top of the fence for two gardens, into the next garden, through a gate, under a broken fence, and into a yard that nobody had done any work in for a long time. One wall was covered with twisted vines of wisteria.

Regina lifted the tangled mass of greenery and revealed a small hiding place.

The two girls slid under the vines and Regina let go. They were completely hidden behind the thick layer of green leaves.

"He'll never find us," Stevie said.

"Sure he will," said Regina. "But not right away. There are only so many hiding places. We all know them well. It's mostly a matter of where he looks first."

That seemed like an odd remark about a place like New York City, but it turned out to be true for the backyard gang, because they'd established rules for fairness. Players weren't allowed to go inside any of the houses and they had to stay within the known backyards. There was an alleyway that led to the street, and they couldn't go there, either.

It took Peter about ten minutes to find them. It took Liza longer to find them during the next round, when they were crouched behind a garden shed at the other end of the block. It took Ann only five minutes to find them on the next round, when they were hidden behind a stack of lawn chairs, but Ann's job was made simpler by the big black poodle that lived in that yard and that sniffed and barked excitedly.

Then it was Gordon's turn to be It. Regina led Stevie to a big bushy rhododendron next to a tall brick wall at the far end of the gardens. The leaves hung down almost as densely as the wisteria had in their first hiding place. There were no sounds of Gordon approaching and no dogs to betray them.

"You really met Skye Ransom?" Regina asked again, settling down on her haunches under the dense greenery.

"Yes, we did. And we've stayed in touch with him," Stevie said. "I mean, it's not like we see him every week or anything, but I guess you'd say we're really his friends."

Regina sighed. "I don't think the other kids believe you."

"I know," Stevie said. "Sometimes I don't believe it myself, but it's true. It's also true that we've gotten him out of some scrapes."

"The handsomest actor in America needs help from a bunch of girls?" Regina asked.

"Not just any bunch," Stevie said. "It's The Saddle Club!" She was teasing, and she could tell Regina knew it. She smiled. "Anyway, even though he is definitely totally handsome, I think he's more interested in my friend Lisa than he is in me."

24

"Bummer."

"I don't think it makes much difference. We're all friends and he's a real person, too. I mean, if he was here, he'd be crouching in this cramped, uncomfortable place just like we are."

"Where's Gordon?" Regina asked.

"Just what I was wondering," Stevie said, glancing at her watch. "Maybe he went home."

"It would be typical," Regina said. "He says he wants to keep up with us, but you know how it is with little kids."

"Yeah, I know," said Stevie, wondering briefly how her friends were doing with Maxi.

"I'm going to check something," Regina said, standing up.

Two seconds later Stevie realized she had no idea where Regina was. But she couldn't have gone far, could she? Stevie peered through the thick foliage. No legs, no feet, no Regina.

She listened. In the distance she could hear the sounds of the city, cars on the other side of the buildings, music emanating from one house, a piano playing in another, and a vacuum cleaner someplace else. She could hear a couple having an argument in a house nearby. A dog barked. Two answered.

"Regina?" Stevie whispered, still reluctant to give away their hiding place, though it was becoming clear that the game was over.

"Regina?" Slowly Stevie stood up and peered through the upper branches of the bush that still shrouded her.

"Regina?" Stevie spoke out loud, now stepping toward the slanting sunlight that told her it was late afternoon. She pushed aside the branches and stepped out into the stranger's backyard where she and Regina had been hidden for half an hour. She looked around at the unfamiliar surroundings. She couldn't remember how they'd gotten there, and she wasn't sure which house was Regina's.

"Regina!" she called out.

No answer.

3

"GET HER!"

Lisa dropped the currycomb she was using and ran. Even as she was doing it, she was aware of the irony that she had to run as fast as she could in order to catch up with a toddler who was merely walking—straight into trouble!

Maxi seemed oblivious to the fact that her goal—Carole's grooming bucket—was on the other side of Belle and that her route was going to take her right under the horse's belly. She could comfortably march underneath the horse even standing at her full height, but Lisa wasn't so certain that Belle would appreciate being used as a tunnel. Belle, Stevie's horse, had been laid low with a sore leg, and Carole and Lisa were giving her special loving attention in Stevie's absence.

Lisa managed to grab Maxi by the waist just before she toddled under the mare's legs.

"Nice catch!" Carole said.

Holding Maxi under one arm, Lisa fetched the portable mounting block and set it down next to Belle. She handed Maxi a chamois and showed her how to rub the horse's smooth coat with the soft cloth.

Sometimes Maxi rubbed the hair in the direction it grew, sometimes she didn't. Fortunately, even with a sore leg, Belle was good-natured. She didn't flinch. She didn't even flinch when Maxi tumbled off the mounting block.

"I knew the riding helmet was a good idea," Lisa said, picking up the little girl and putting her back on the block.

Carole smiled. "Well, she's got enough padding on her other landing site, doesn't she?" she asked, looking at the thick diaper-and-pants covering that protected Maxi's bottom whenever she fell down.

"She's so cute," Lisa said, regarding their little charge.

28

"Yes, but as Max noticed, she's a slight distraction if you're trying to get anything else done."

"Like horse care or instruction or stable management."

"Anything," Carole repeated.

They had been trying to groom Belle for over an hour.

"REGINA!" STEVIE TRIED to control the panic in her voice, but she found herself overwhelmed with the kinds of fears her mother always talked about having. She started remembering everything bad she'd ever heard about children lost in the city. Regina might have been mugged or, worse, kidnapped. She could be being held hostage by international terrorists. Stevie's mind was working so fast that she was already trying to figure out how to raise the ransom money when she thought she heard a sound.

"Regina?" she called out again.

There was no answer. But there was a shuffling sound. *It could be the kidnappers. It could be the muggers. It could be murderers or marauders or whatever bad guys there are that hang around backyards in New York.*

There was another sound—a snort, a snuffle. The

sound of a giggle being stifled. Ah, perhaps it was the work of the rogue band of ticklers! Stevie found herself not as worried but a lot more curious. She looked around, trying to judge where the sound had come from.

She was standing by a brick wall that abutted an old greenhouse. All the glass panes had been shattered, their ruins covering the abandoned greenhouse floor. The ghostly remains of the window frames were chipped and worn. Inside among the glass shards were long rows of boards on blocks, the former resting place of hundreds of potted plants. Stevie went inside. There was no sign of Regina, but Stevie was certain that this was where the giggles had come from. The greenhouse was attached to an old brownstone, the building at the farthest end of the block. Stevie remembered seeing it from the street because it was boarded up and had signs warning people away and notices that a licensed contractor was doing work on it. At least she knew where she was now.

At the back of the empty greenhouse, Stevie saw a door to the boarded-up house. It was boarded up, too, but there was something suspicious about the boards.

Stevie walked over and tested them. They didn't swing out as a door would, but they swung up ever so slightly.

"Regina?" Stevie called into the shadows beyond.

A hand darted out of the darkness and slapped Stevie's hand sharply.

"Tag! You're It!"

For a split second Stevie was stunned and confused. Then she realized she'd been at the receiving end of a practical joke. Being a natural-born practical joker herself, she wasn't always at her best when she was on the receiving end, but in this case she was so relieved to find that Regina was there, not being tortured or held for ransom, and was accompanied by Ann, Liza, Peter, and Gordon, that she simply laughed. She proceeded into the dark room and looked around.

"We knew you'd find us!" Regina said.

Any trace of anger Stevie might have still felt over the joke disappeared when Regina paid her that compliment.

"What a cool place!" Stevie declared when her eyes became accustomed to the darkness.

"It sure is," Liza agreed.

They were standing on the ground floor near the kitchen, in what had probably been the dining room of the original house. It was dusty and empty except for bits of trash here and there and a small pile of bricks. There were four unopened buckets of drywall compound, which Stevie could tell would be put to good use eventually.

"Let's go upstairs," Regina said, leading the group up an elegant staircase with a wide banister.

At the top of the staircase was a large room the size of the whole house, except for a small closed-off area that Stevie suspected had been or would be a half bathroom. The large room was divided by an enormous archway, which seemed to have held double doors at one time. There were windows on either end, all boarded up now. One would overlook the street, the other the greenhouse and backyard. Cracks in the boards over the windows allowed Stevie to see the room in a dim gray light. The walls and ceiling had elaborate plaster moldings around them, though there were sections that were damaged or missing. There was an outlet for a chandelier in the center of each half of the room. It wasn't hard to imagine the room's former splendor. Stevie thought of women in silk dresses with lace and bustles having polite conversations with men in tailcoated suits by the marble fireplace.

"Really cool," Stevie said.

"And somebody's going to make it cool again," said Ann, pointing to the pile of construction material in one corner of the front room. She and Peter started moving crates of floor tiles into a semicircle around the fireplace so that they could sit on them.

"Are we allowed to be in here?" Stevie asked. She looked around at the other kids for an answer, but nobody spoke—an answer in itself.

Peter looked at his watch. "It's getting kind of late now," he said. "Maybe we should meet back here another time?"

"To tell ghost stories?" Stevie suggested.

"Exactly!" Liza agreed.

"Do you know any?" Regina asked her.

"Not very many," Stevie said humbly. "But the ones I know are really, really scary. Probably too scary for this group. I mean, I just wouldn't want—"

"Yeah, right!" said Peter. "Just try us!"

"I will," Stevie said.

33

The kids all made a plan to meet back there the next afternoon.

"Three o'clock sharp," Regina said.

Everyone agreed.

Quickly, without disturbing anything else, the group exited the same way Stevie had come in, through the greenhouse door, and dispersed to their own homes. By the time Stevie was teetering along the brick wall that led to Regina's backyard, she felt completely at ease. She was really getting to love New York—and it was a part of New York she'd never known existed.

At dinner that night Mrs. Lake spoke excitedly about the business meeting she'd had. The legal talk was totally over Stevie's head, but she understood that her mother was pleased with the way things were going, and that was good news because it meant they'd be staying with Regina and her mother for at least the rest of the week.

"And what were you two up to?" Mrs. Lake asked.

"This is the coolest place, Mom," Stevie said, matching her mother's excitement about New York with her own. "There are really neat kids around here and Regina knows them all. We were playing in the backyards."

"You go onto other people's property?" Mrs. Lake asked.

"It's like it's everyone's," Stevie said.

"The neighbors understand," said Mrs. Evans. "As long as the kids don't do any damage."

"We're careful," said Regina.

"Most of the time," Mrs. Evans said.

"Well, we never go through Mr. Simon's yard anymore," said Regina.

"Tomato plants," said Mrs. Evans by way of explanation.

"There are lots of places to play cool games," said Stevie. "We even—"

"We were playing hide-and-seek," Regina cut in.

Stevie realized that Regina had thought she was going to say something about going into the house with the greenhouse. She never would have done that.

"Just what I was going to say," said Stevie. "We were hiding behind some vines and nobody could see us at all."

"For a while," said Regina.

"You didn't bother anyone, did you?" Mrs. Evans asked.

"Nobody at all," said Regina.

"I heard the poodle barking," said Mrs. Evans.

"He always does that. It was nothing. Really, nothing."

Mrs. Evans looked up at Stevie's mother. "Catherine, I'm a little worried that Regina may not be the best influence. . . ."

Stevie stifled a giggle. Her mother came to the rescue with a smile. "Don't worry, Elisa," she said. "And please don't be misled by Stevie's angelic face. When it comes to bad influences—"

"Mom, can we go to a museum tomorrow?" Regina interrupted. She apparently knew when a conversation was taking an undesirable turn. Stevie was relieved on her own behalf, though she was secretly flattered that her mother had described her as having an angelic face. She'd already been feeling good that Regina had had confidence that Stevie could find the group when they were hiding in the house, and now her mother thought she was an angel, or at least looked like one. That was two compliments in one day!

"Which museum?" Mrs. Evans asked.

"Natural history?" Regina suggested.

"Oh, the dinosaurs!" Stevie said. "Let's do it."

"I won't have time to take you," said Mrs. Lake. "And I'm sure Elisa won't, either."

36

"It's not a problem, Catherine," said Regina's mother. "The museum is an easy bus ride, and I know Regina can get there by herself. I think the girls would enjoy the adventure. Wouldn't you?"

"Definitely," Stevie agreed.

"And you'll be careful?" Stevie's mother asked.

"Aren't I always?" Stevie asked. Then she thought better of it. "Maybe you shouldn't answer that!"

Mrs. Lake laughed. "You're not always careful," she said. "But you always seem to manage to come out on top. Somehow."

"Well, that's good enough, isn't it?" Stevie asked.

Her mother didn't answer.

ONE OF THE things Stevie thought was really great about New York was how she and Regina could just go someplace on a bus. No car, no parents, no brothers—just go! Taking the bus across town in New York City was no bigger deal for Regina than biking to a friend's house in Willow Creek was for Stevie. Here she was in one of the biggest cities in the world and she and Regina were on their own. Naturally they had to call Regina's mother when they got to the museum, and they had to promise about sixteen times that they'd be careful.

The museum was full of people. They were mostly families with kids, but there were also kids with groups and kids with friends. It was soon clear to Stevie that Regina had spent a lot of time visiting that museum and knew her way around very well. They saw the dinosaurs, all right. They also saw rooms full of African and then Asian animals. Stevie's favorite exhibit was the herd of stuffed elephants. In one corner of her mind, she knew somebody had hunted those elephants and killed them. That fact made her sad, but the group of them was so real that it almost felt as if she were in the middle of the African plains. While she hated the idea of all those animals being killed, she told herself that it had happened a long time ago and that at least their deaths hadn't been wasted. She, along with millions of other kids and adults, had the privilege of seeing them as if they were still alive.

"Okay, I'm ready to go," said Regina.

"Back on the bus?" Stevie asked.

"Nah, let's walk."

"Across the park?" Stevie asked. "Your mom'll kill us, and if she doesn't, mine will."

"It's broad daylight," Regina reminded Stevie. "And it's a nice day. Besides, you told me that you and your friends rode horses in the park by yourselves. If you can ride a horse there, you shouldn't be worried about walking there."

Stevie wasn't so sure about that. She always felt safer on a horse than on foot. But she also agreed with Regina that the park was probably pretty safe in the bright sunshine.

It turned out to be perfectly safe. The two girls walked past playgrounds, softball fields, chess players, picnickers, and, Stevie thought, about a thousand dogs. They walked past the bridle path onto an adjoining footpath.

"There! That's the place. I remember it exactly!" Stevie said.

"What place?" asked Regina.

"The place where Skye Ransom fell off his horse," Stevie explained.

Regina walked over to the spot Stevie indicated. She crouched down and ran her open hand over the patch of grass. "You mean I'm touching the grass that Skye Ransom's rear was on?" she asked. Her voice dripped with skepticism. Stevie knew Regina didn't believe it had really happened, but it had and there seemed to be nothing she could do to convince Regina of that, so she played along with her.

"Actually, it was more like his chin was there. His knees were here. . . ." Stevie smiled. "Yeah," she said. "And his butt was there. X marks the spot."

"Oooooh!" Regina teased. She stood up. "Come on, let's get some ice cream."

Stevie was relieved that the subject was closed. The way Regina said it told her that she still didn't believe her but wasn't going to call her a liar. More important, they were still friends.

"My treat," Stevie said. "Well, Mom's treat." She took out the money her mother had given her that morning.

An hour later the girls were back at Regina's house, telling Mrs. Evans about all the things they'd seen at the museum. Regina made a point of saying that both bus trips had been totally uneventful. Mrs. Evans seemed pleased with the report. Stevie thought it hadn't been necessary to add the part about *both* bus trips. She herself was more than capable of leaving out extraneous information that would not necessarily make her mother happy, but she wasn't awfully good at an out-and-out lie. Still, they'd had no problems walking back. Maybe Regina knew what she was doing.

"C'mon," said Regina. "We've got to get out of here."

"Why?"

"We were supposed to meet everybody at three o'clock. Remember?"

Stevie had almost forgotten. She looked at her watch. It was already quarter after three.

She ran up to Regina's room, which overlooked the garden, and stowed the bag of postcards and the realistic rubber snake she'd bought just in case she ever had a good use for it (she'd had her brother Michael in mind) and met Regina in the backyard five minutes later. Five minutes after that they were scrunching across the rubble and broken glass in the greenhouse to get into the boarded-up brownstone.

"Hello?" Regina called from the old dining room on the ground floor.

There was no answer at first. The two girls went over to the staircase, thinking their friends would have gone back up to the parlor floor, where they'd been the day before, but they weren't there.

"I bet they're downstairs," Regina said, signaling Stevie to follow her.

At the back of the staircase was a little door that had been left open a crack. Regina pulled the door back farther and peered inside.

"Quick! Get down here!" a voice whispered from the darkness.

Regina didn't waste any time. She slid through the door and Stevie followed right after her.

It wasn't completely dark. A dim light shone from a single bulb in the middle of the basement ceiling. Peter, Liza, Ann, and Gordon were all huddled under it, sitting on boxes that looked as if they'd spent the last century down there.

Peter had his finger to his lips, indicating that Stevie and Regina should be quiet. Stevie couldn't imagine why, but the look of terror on Gordon's face told her that there was a reason.

"Someone's upstairs," Ann whispered, barely audible.

Stevie sat down on the box next to Liza and listened. Someone *was* upstairs. She and Regina must have come into the back of the house just after someone else had come into the front. They could hear footsteps on the front steps leading up to the house's main entrance on the parlor floor. There was the click of a key turning in the lock.

"Must be the guy who's working on the house," Peter said.

"It's about the first time he's been here in months," said Ann.

"Could be the end of our fun," Peter observed.

"Are they going to find us?" Gordon asked.

"Not if I have anything to say about it," Peter said. He put his arm around the younger boy's shoulders. It was a small gesture, but a sweet and protective one. Stevie realized she liked Peter. Not that it was going to make any difference if they all got caught and spent the rest of their young lives in a detention center.

"Aren't we trespassing?" Stevie whispered.

"Her parents are both lawyers," Regina explained.

Liza giggled. Stevie didn't.

The footsteps were now definitely in the house. There seemed to be a couple of people up there. Judging by the weight of the steps, Stevie figured they were men. That made sense. Most construction workers were men.

"Hey, Frank! Look at this. Some stuff's been moved around."

Stevie felt a chill on the back of her neck. The boxes upstairs.

"Kids!" another voice exclaimed.

"How'd they get in here?"

"Must've broken their way in. We'll find out where."

Nobody in the basement moved for the next ten

44

minutes. They heard the two men tromp around the house. They heard them bringing some things in. Everything went straight up to the parlor floor.

Sitting there in the dim light, Stevie looked around her. The basement seemed small compared to the basement in her own house. Also, it hadn't been built with any other use in mind than to house a furnace and water heater. The ceiling was high, but no attempt had been made to make it a pleasant place to be. There was a small open area where they were sitting—and then Stevie noticed something that seemed completely out of place, because it was totally new and very clean. It was a closet of sorts, built into one corner of the cellar.

Stevie's eyes rested on the odd plywood closet. It was as high as the ceiling and perhaps eight feet long and six feet wide. Odder than the fact that it was there at all, though, was the door, which was latched not with one or two but with three padlocks.

She pointed at it and made a face. Regina looked where she was pointing and shrugged.

"Who knows?" she mused.

Stevie knew that construction materials could be expensive—her mother had certainly complained enough about the cost when the Lakes had redone their kitchen the previous year—but nothing that they used was so expensive it had to be locked up.

Stevie shrugged, too. Whatever was in there was none of her business.

"Frank! Look at this!"

The sound was almost right over their heads. The men were in the dining room on the ground floor. Stevie held her breath.

"Well, I'll be . . ." Frank said. "Kids," he repeated. "Get the hammer and nails. They won't get in here again!"

The kids all exchanged looks. At that very moment, getting *in* was the last thing on their minds! To their horror they heard the sounds of very big nails being pounded into the door from the greenhouse to the dining room.

Nobody spoke. They just looked at one another, and Peter kept holding Gordon around his shoulders.

The only good news was that the men made no attempt to see if any kids were still in the house. As soon as they pounded the nails into the back door, they left by the front one, locking it behind them, and then, as the kids listened, fastening a padlock onto it as well.

They were locked in tight.

As soon as the footsteps receded down the stairs and the trespassers heard slamming car doors and the sound of a car engine turning over, Gordon burst into tears.

Liza gave him a dirty look.

"Don't worry, Gordon," Peter said. "We'll find a way out, and with any luck it'll be a new way for us to get in."

"Are you crazy?" Gordon asked.

"Just a little bit," said Peter. That made Gordon laugh, and his laughter made everybody feel a little bit better.

"Right, and when we come back, we can figure out what's in that closet," Regina said, pointing to the padlocked plywood box in the corner.

"Are *you* crazy?" Liza asked.

"Well, we certainly can't do it now," Regina said. "It's broad daylight and there are too many people up on the street who might hear the noise if we tried to break the padlocks."

"And some other time will be different?" Liza asked, apparently still trying to absorb the idea that Regina was proposing they break into somebody else's locked storage area.

"Well, sure," said Regina. "See, the padlocks are all combination locks."

47

"Yes?"

"And when we come back tonight to tell ghost stories—we *are* coming back tonight to tell ghost stories, aren't we?" She looked around.

"If we ever get out of here in order to be able to come back," Peter said.

"Of course we will," Regina said, dismissing his concern with a wave of her hand. "So, when we come back, you guys can bring one of your father's stethoscopes. That's how you can hear when the tumblers click in a combination lock. I mean, we all know it works for safes, so of course it's got to work for these piddly padlocks, right?"

Nobody was disagreeing with her. Stevie had already noticed that nobody ever disagreed with Regina. The girl was always so certain about things that it was impossible to argue with her.

"Okay, so then it's settled. But first we have to find a new way to get in."

Almost anybody else in the world would have described it as a new way to get out. Stevie could hardly help laughing, at least to herself.

The kids all stood up and began looking around. It turned out not to be difficult at all. It was practically in front of their noses. There was a small window just below the ceiling in the basement. It had some boards over it, but the foundation of the house was concrete, so the contractor had simply propped the boards up against it. Peter stacked enough abandoned boxes so that he could climb up to the window, open it, and shove at the boards. The boards fell aside.

They had to stack all the old boxes up against the wall so that even Gordon, the shortest of them, could reach the window, but within a few minutes they were outside, propping the boards back up.

"Okay then, how about eight o'clock tonight?" Regina proposed. "And bring flashlights!"

"Right," came an unenthusiastic response from Ann. Being locked in the basement and terrified of being discovered had not seemed to have whetted anybody's appetite for a return visit, even to a cool place like the old house.

"Come on, guys!" Regina said. "You're not afraid of a few construction guys, are you?"

"I am," said Gordon. "What if they'd found us?"

"Ah, but they didn't!" Regina said triumphantly. "And besides, Stevie knows these wonderful ghost stories that she's dying to tell us!"

There was still hesitation.

"And I'll bring marshmallows."

That seemed to do it.

"Eight o'clock it is!" they said.

Stevie looked at her watch. Eight o'clock didn't seem anywhere near long enough away.

"MAXI! COME HERE, Maxi! Come to Lisa!"

It wasn't working at all. Maxi clearly didn't have the slightest interest in doing anything Lisa suggested. Instead she tried to run after the ponies and horses. The only good news about that was that there weren't any around at the moment, for she surely would have ended up under the hooves of one of them.

"I'm beginning to think that looking after Maxi is a big job," Lisa admitted to Carole, who was trying to head the toddler off before she climbed over a jump that was set up for the afternoon adult jump class.

"I always thought it was," Carole said. "And I will always remember that this was your bright idea."

"Guilty," Lisa admitted. "But as long as we're looking after her, Max can get some work done."

"Even though it's our vacation, we don't seem to be getting much riding done," Carole reminded her.

"But we're pitching in to help someone out," Lisa said. "And that's one of The Saddle Club rules."

"Sure," Carole agreed. "But the people we're supposed to help out first is The Saddle Club!"

"And what about all the money we're earning? You don't think that's helping out?"

Carole didn't answer. She was too busy shifting to the left as fast as she could to block Maxi's access to the jump. She picked up the toddler and gave her a hug.

Maxi didn't hug back. In fact, she kicked and howled. Carole knew if she put her down, the little girl would just take off, heading into something even more dangerous than the jump she'd wanted to climb.

"Maybe we should take her inside," Carole suggested.

"Oh, sure," Lisa said. "Remember how much she wanted to climb the manure pile a half hour ago? That's why we're out here."

Carole did remember. She put Maxi down and took her hand. Lisa took the other one. Together the girls could pick Maxi up and swing her. Maxi liked that. She liked it so much that both Lisa and Carole soon found themselves with sore backs from leaning over.

"How about a nap?" Carole said to Maxi as cheerfully as she could, hoping to make it sound like as much fun for Maxi as it would be for the two of them to have a little rest from baby chasing.

"No nap!" Maxi declared. The little girl didn't talk much, but she obviously knew that word when she heard it.

Lisa couldn't help herself: She laughed. Carole sighed.

"Hi, girls, how's it going?" Mrs. Reg asked, emerging from the barn.

"We're exhausted and it's only been a little over an hour so far today," Carole said.

"She reminds me of her father when he was a little boy," said Mrs. Reg.

Carole and Lisa exchanged looks. It was hard to imagine Max as a little boy, especially as a toddler.

"He was this energetic?" Lisa asked.

"Oh yes," said Mrs. Reg. "I thought my back would break from chasing after him and picking him up. He was always fascinated by the manure pile. It was all I could do to keep him out of it."

"We know what that's like," Lisa said.

"I guess it's in the genes," Mrs. Reg said. "And now my son has the child he deserves, except you're paying the price today!"

They all laughed at that.

Mrs. Reg picked up her granddaughter and gave her a little hug before sitting down on the mounting block. "Being a handful, are we?" she asked. Maxi blinked her eyes and smiled at Mrs. Reg. The look was so utterly angelic that it was almost hard to remember that this very same little girl had been aiming to yank Patch's tail a mere half hour earlier. Maxi settled into her grandmother's lap.

"We used to have a stallion here, you know," said Mrs. Reg. Her eyes got a familiar faraway look that told Carole and Lisa she was about to tell them one of her tales. Mrs. Reg's stories were often confusing to the girls, and Mrs. Reg would never explain exactly why she'd decided to tell the story. Carole and Lisa leaned against the fence and did the only thing they could do, which was listen.

"I forget the stallion's name, but he was a handful and Max—*my* Max . . ." She emphasized the *my*. That meant she was referring to Max's father, who had died some time ago. The girls usually referred to him as Max the Second, because he was the second Maximilian Regnery to own Pine Hollow. The current Max was Max the Third. "Well, my Max didn't know what to do with him. He started him out in that paddock." She pointed to the paddock nearest the schooling ring. It was small but pleasant, with some grass and a nice enough view of the stable and riding rings to satisfy the curiosity of most horses.

"What happened?" Lisa asked. Mrs. Reg scowled. It was a mistake to interrupt her, even with a question, when she was telling one of her stories. "Sorry," Lisa said quickly.

"He jumped the fence. Went right into the field beyond."

Carole and Lisa looked where Mrs. Reg was pointing. The fence around that paddock was higher than any of the other fences at Pine Hollow. They didn't mention that, though. They waited for Mrs. Reg to continue.

"So Max built the fence up higher. I bet you've always wondered why that fence was higher than the others, haven't you?"

"Sure," said Lisa.

"Absolutely," said Carole. In fact, the thought had never crossed either of their minds until that minute.

"Well, that's why," said Mrs. Reg. "And that old stallion would just run around that paddock, itchy, annoyed, and very unhappy—always trying to get out. He'd get up against the part of the fence next to the field and rear up on his hind legs, whinnying and bucking, behaving just like the naughtiest little child you ever saw. That stallion had a tantrum every time he went into the paddock."

There was a long pause. Mrs. Reg tickled Maxi, who giggled and then put her head on her grandmother's shoulder. Lisa wished she could get Maxi to be that tame with her. Grandmothers were different from baby-sitters, though, and even Lisa knew that. She and Carole waited.

"Then one day that no-good stable hand we had back then—I've forgotten his name, too, and that's all for the best—he did what he often did. He forgot to close the gate."

That was hard to imagine since one of the first rules anybody learned about being around any kind of livestock, and especially horses, was to latch every gate behind you. No wonder Mrs. Reg had forgotten his name.

56

Mrs. Reg stood up and handed Maxi back to Lisa. Maxi immediately wiggled out of Lisa's grasp and started heading for the stable. Images of Maxi and the manure pile inclined Lisa to follow her. Curiosity held her back for a moment.

"What happened to the stallion?" Lisa asked.

Mrs. Reg shook her head as if the answer were utterly obvious. "Happy as a clam of course," she said. "We never had a minute's trouble with him after that, and he spent the rest of his days with us out in the field."

Mrs. Reg strode toward the barn, then called back over her shoulder, "You girls better get in here! I think Maxi wants to get into Nickel's stall!"

Carole and Lisa dashed after the little girl and stopped her right before she unlatched the pony's stall door. Nickel had a sweet nature, but he was still a lot bigger than Maxi.

Lisa tucked the wiggling little girl under one arm and turned to Carole, who seemed in a hurry to get to the tack room.

"What was that all about?" she asked, referring to Mrs. Reg's story.

"Maxi, of course," said Carole.

"You think she wants to jump a fence and go into the field?" Lisa asked.

"Of course not," said Carole. "She wants to ride!"

"And you think it's a good idea?" Lisa asked.

"It's not my idea," said Carole. "It's Mrs. Reg's. Don't you see?"

And then Lisa did see. Maxi was just like the stallion. She'd be much happier if they let her do what she really wanted, which was to ride. And as long as they saw to it that she rode safely, she'd be much safer than when she was running around in schooling rings or trying to open stall doors.

"Right!" said Lisa. "Sure she wants to ride. It's in her blood. Anybody named Regnery would be happier on a horse than anyplace else, right?"

"Right," Carole agreed.

It took the two of them just a few minutes to tack up Penny, the stable's smallest pony. Maxi, seeming to sense that this was about her, sat patiently on a bale of hay and watched the girls work. Carole got a lead rope, then Lisa lifted the little girl and put her in the saddle, securing her riding helmet before settling her in. She adjusted the stirrups to their shortest length, which was exactly right for Maxi's short legs. The look on Maxi's face was pure joy when the pony began to move forward.

Their first stop was at the stable's good-luck horse-shoe, where they showed Maxi how to touch it for luck. They each gave it a swipe, too, since the little girl's safety was more in their hands than in her own. Maxi seemed oblivious to any possible dangers of riding. She held the reins as if she knew exactly what she was doing and waited for the girls to get Penny moving.

It didn't take long. Carole led the pony at a gentle walk while Lisa walked next to the saddle, being sure at every step that Maxi was secure in it. She needn't have worried. Maxi behaved as if she'd been born to be in a saddle, which seemed about right when Lisa thought about it.

They'd gone around the ring five times at a sedate walk and Maxi was showing no signs of wanting to stop when Deborah's car pulled into the driveway.

Neither Carole nor Lisa saw the car, but Maxi did.

"Mommy!" she cried out.

Lisa's heart sank as she realized that she and Carole were letting Deborah's daughter do something that Deborah might very well not approve of. Deborah wasn't horse-crazy. She didn't exactly hate horses, and she wasn't as afraid of them as she had been when she first met Max, but she'd never really learned to love horses the way Max and Mrs. Reg did. Maybe it would have been a good idea for Lisa and Carole to get her permission before putting Maxi on Penny.

Lisa and Carole looked over at Deborah. She stood by the open door of her car. Her face was pale with worry. Lisa was about to say something. She wasn't sure exactly what she was going to say, but she was about to open her mouth when Maxi spoke for all of them.

"Look at me!" she cried with delight.

Deborah closed her mouth and sighed. She walked over to the young equestrienne.

"Are you having a good time?" she asked.

Maxi's smile was all the answer anyone needed. The little girl kicked gently at the pony's belly, getting her to move along at her easy walk.

Deborah looked at Lisa and Carole. "Thanks, girls," she said.

"You're welcome," Lisa told her.

"We're being careful," Carole added.

"I can see that," said Deborah. She picked up her computer and briefcase and headed for the house. "I'll see you later, Maxi!" she told her daughter, but the

little girl's attention was already totally turned
to the job at hand, which was riding Penny. She
seemed to have completely forgotten about her
mother.

"It's in the genes," Carole said.

"AND HOW WAS the museum?" Mrs. Lake asked Stevie. It took her more than a minute to figure out that her mother was asking about the natural history museum. It seemed like an awfully long time ago that she and Regina had been there—at least one near disaster ago!

"It was great!" Stevie said. "Dinosaurs, you know."

"I know," said her mother.

"And elephants. I liked the elephants."

The two girls and their mothers were all sitting at dinner in the Evanses' dining room. Like the dining room at the old house, it was on the ground floor and looked out on the backyard.

"How was your day, Mom?" Stevie asked.

"Dinosaurs and elephants would have been an improvement," she said. "A big one. Well, it wasn't that bad, actually, but I just wish these people would be more reasonable."

"You mean like they should see it your way?" Stevie teased.

"Exactly," said her mother. "I mean, we're going to finish our business, but they're making it take so long!"

"Sounds like good news to me," Regina said. "The longer they take, the longer Stevie can stay here, right?"

"As long as you two don't get into any major trouble," said Mrs. Evans.

"Whatever would make you think something like that?" Regina asked. Her mother just gave her a look that pretty much said it all. Stevie was beginning to think that Regina spent more time in hot water than she did, and after this afternoon she thought she knew why.

"So, what's everybody up to this evening?" Mrs. Evans asked.

"A hot bath and bed," said Stevie's mother. Being a lawyer was hard work sometimes, Stevie knew, though her mother often said that being a mother was even harder.

"Girls?" Mrs. Evans asked.

"We're going over to Ann and Peter's. We're going to meet the gang there. Stevie claims to know some really good ghost stories."

Mrs. Lake laughed. "She does. She sometimes tries to tell them at dinner and freak out her brothers. Alex and Chad never seem to mind, but Michael has been known to run from the table."

"That's why ghost stories have been outlawed from the dinner table," Stevie explained. "But that's okay. It's better if I tell them in the car, when Michael can't run anywhere!"

"Well," said Mrs. Evans, "it's okay to go to Peter's, but don't be late, okay? Catherine and I are really tired and we're likely to be asleep before you get home, but the curfew is still ten P.M. sharp."

"That's okay, Mom. We'll be home by then, won't we, Stevie?"

"Oh, sure," Stevie said, but at that moment her mother's plan was feeling like a better one than Regina's. Bath and bed versus breaking and entering. "By ten, easy," she promised.

After dinner the girls cleared the table, then

Mrs. Evans told them it was okay to go on over to Peter's. Regina had lots to do before they could leave, and she got Stevie to help her fill her school backpack. They needed candles, a flashlight for each of them, and lots of snacks, including marshmallows, chocolate milk, cheese crackers, and diet soda.

The mothers surveyed the girls' snack choices with raised eyebrows. Mrs. Evans handed Regina a stack of paper cups so that they wouldn't have to use Peter's mother's glasses.

"Good idea," said Regina. "She'll be really grateful for that."

"She'll be grateful if you don't make nuisances of yourselves in her home," said Mrs. Evans.

Stevie wished they were planning to make nuisances of themselves in Peter's home instead of in the old house. There was no turning Regina back, though. She considered her plan a done deal. Stevie was beginning to see it as her job to keep Regina from doing something really ridiculous, like breaking into the locked storage closet.

"We're out of here. G'night, Mom," said Regina, giving her mother a quick peck on the cheek.

"At ten o'clock sharp I want you to come in and tell

me you're home safe and sound, even if you have to wake me up. Understand, Regina?"

"I understand, Mom. Of course I will. I promise."

"Have fun, girls," said Stevie's mother.

"We will," said Stevie.

With that, the two of them went out the garden door. Mrs. Evans turned on the garden light for them, and it would stay on until they got home and turned it off themselves. Both Mrs. Evans's room and the room where Stevie's mother was staying were on the front side of the house. They would not be bothered by the light in the backyard.

The girls climbed up onto the fence and then looked back to wave to their mothers, but the two women had already left the kitchen, presumably headed for their hot baths.

"This way!" Regina said, leading Stevie along the brick wall.

When they got to the old house, Peter was just ahead of them at the basement window.

"Good evening, ladies," he said, greeting them as if he were a doorman. He held the boards to the side while they lowered themselves in, then he followed and replaced the boards. The dim ceiling light was turned on, so they knew someone else was already there.

"Hello!" Regina called, just above a whisper.

Gordon appeared from the other side of the closet.

"We were just checking this out," said Gordon. "There's no way in at all. We couldn't even see through the cracks with a flashlight." He held up a flashlight as if to show that they'd tried.

"We'll work on it later," said Regina. "First we need to tell some good ghost stories. Where's the best place for that?"

"We could stay here," Stevie suggested, comforted by the idea that as long as they were in the basement, they were only a few short steps from escape.

"Too dirty," said Peter.

"Too ugly," said Ann.

"Okay, where?" Regina asked again.

"I like the parlor floor," Peter said. "I like the tall ceilings and the big marble fireplace. Maybe we could even light a fire in it."

"I'm sure it's been closed off for years," Regina said.

"Well, then maybe we could put some candles in it and pretend we've got a fire. You brought candles, didn't you?"

"Of course I did," Regina said. "And Stevie packed some marshmallows that we can cook over them."

"Cool!" said Gordon. "Just like camp!"

"All we need are graham crackers and chocolate bars," Peter said.

"I brought raisins," said Ann.

"Where's Liza?" Peter asked.

"Beats me," said Regina.

"She was kind of freaked this afternoon," Ann told the group. "I wouldn't be surprised if she doesn't come tonight. She said something about having to go somewhere with her mother, but I don't know if that's true."

"That's okay," said Regina. "It's no fun if someone's really scared. She'll be back with us another time."

Two thoughts entered Stevie's head. The first was that it was nice of Regina to respect the fact that Liza was nervous, and that she didn't seem to think less of her for it. The second was that she wished she'd told Regina how freaked she was so that *she* could have stayed home! Well, it was too late for that now.

"Do you know really scary stories?" Gordon asked Stevie.

"The scariest," Regina answered for her. "Even her mother says so."

"Let's go, then," Peter said, heading for the stairs.

The house looked very different at night. There was no light at all coming through the cracks in the boards over the windows. As the flashlight beams crisscrossed on the stairs and in the hallway, Stevie found herself staring at the dancing shadows they cast on the walls and floors. It was pure inspiration for a ghost story expert like Stevie Lake. She was getting ready to scare the daylights out of all of them. And they'd love every minute of it. Things were looking up. A little.

It took a few minutes to set up their story circle. They pulled boxes back around the fireplace, set some candles in it, then set even more in a semicircle around the hearth. Stevie took the seat of honor, facing the fireplace.

A great deal of food was produced. Regina set out some of their goodies, including the marshmallows, but she kept the cheese crackers and chocolate milk until later.

Ann passed around her big bag of raisins, which

everybody enjoyed. Gordon offered them all a drink of his blue fruit punch. They all said no thank you to that, favoring instead Peter's apple juice.

"Ah, thirteen candles!" Stevie began. "A perfect number for a night like tonight, for it was exactly the number of candles that Lady Griselda lit on her husband's bier the night her head fell off."

She paused for dramatic effect. In the moment of silence, she heard two truck doors slam right in front of the house.

"Did you bring the key?" a too-familiar voice demanded from the street, just on the other side of the boarded-up windows. It was the same man who had been there in the afternoon: Frank.

"What kind of idiot do you think I am?" said the other man.

"You don't want me to answer that, Maurice," Frank said.

He clearly hadn't said it to be funny. These guys were mean and they weren't going to be pleased to find the *kids* back again.

"Hide!" Regina said.

Good idea, but where? thought Stevie. As fast as they could, the group blew out all the candles. They couldn't go up higher in the house because the staircase to the next floor didn't have any stairs on it. It would be treacherous in broad daylight and deadly in the dark.

The group clustered behind a stack of wooden planks and did everything they could to stop breathing, or at least to stop sounding as if they were breathing. Stevie wondered if the pounding in her chest could be heard downstairs. She suspected that it could.

Next to her, Stevie could feel that Gordon's knees were shaking and he was shivering. Once again she saw Peter take the little boy's shoulders and hold them for comfort. She was just beginning to wonder where her own comfort was going to come from when she felt Regina grab her around the waist. It didn't exactly make her feel better, but it let her know that Regina did, in fact, have some nerves after all. There was some comfort in that. She put her own arm around Ann's shoulders.

"Come on! Bring that stuff down here!" Frank bellowed.

Maurice hauled something into the house and, mercifully, downstairs instead of up.

"Hey, the light's on!" Maurice said.

The kids looked around at one another. Had they really left it on?

"I left it on," Peter whispered. "So we could find our way out."

Stevie could have sworn her knees were knocking. It turned out to be Gordon's knee knocking against hers.

"Yeah, well, you must have left it on last time!" said Frank. "Remember who's paying the electricity bill!"

"Sure, for this twenty-five-watt bulb. Big deal," said Maurice.

He made two more trips down to the basement while Frank grumbled about how slow he was.

"Okay, that's it," said Maurice.

"Did you lock it up good?"

"I locked it up good," Maurice answered. "And I turned off the light to save you some precious money, like you need any help in that department."

"Let's stop the chitchat and get out of here," Frank said.

The door slammed. There was the now familiar sound of the key in the lock and then in the padlock. Footsteps down the stairs. Truck doors opening. Truck doors slamming. The engine turning over. The sound of the truck fading into the distance.

"Ah-chooooooo!" It was Ann.

It was such a totally weird sound after their silent terror that all the kids started laughing, except Gordon. He cried. And then he laughed. Again, Peter hugged him. So did Stevie and Regina, and finally Ann, once she'd sneezed twice more.

"That's it!" said Regina.

Stevie's thought exactly. She was more than ready to go home.

"We've just *got* to find out what's in that closet!" Regina said, continuing her thought. That wasn't what Stevie'd had in mind at all.

"I mean, what could be so important that it has to be delivered practically in the middle of the night and then locked up with three padlocks?"

It was a good question, but it wasn't one Stevie was absolutely sure she wanted to answer.

"Listen, could we maybe—" she began.

"I brought the stethoscope," said Peter, pulling it out of his pocket. "I don't know how to tell when a lock is unlocking, though."

"They do it on TV all the time," said Regina. "It can't be all that hard."

Stevie was inclined to remind Regina that TV was fiction and this was real life, but she had the feeling Regina wasn't in a reality mode. She was in a curiosity mode, and the only way to get out of curiosity mode was to satisfy the curiosity.

Stevie switched on the flashlight and led the kids back down to the basement. At least there they would be close to the exit, to safety.

It didn't work. Or at least they didn't know how to make it work. Regina made Peter hold the stethoscope over the back of the padlock while she listened and turned the dial. Stevie held the flashlight. She didn't want to risk turning on the overhead light again.

"Left first, right?" asked Regina.

"No, right then left," said Peter.

She twirled it to the right. She shook her head. She twirled it slowly. Nothing. She tried left.

"What's that?" Ann asked.

"Nothing," said Regina.

"No, I heard something," said Ann.

"There's no sound here," said Regina. "I can't hear a darn thing!"

"I thought I did, too," said Peter.

74

"Be quiet!" said Regina, concentrating on the padlock.

Everybody was quiet. And then everybody heard
another sound. It didn't come from the padlock. It
came from outside.

"Do you hear that?" Lisa asked.

"What?" Carole asked.

"That's it," said Lisa.

"I don't hear anything."

"Isn't it wonderful?" asked Lisa, sighing.

Carole smiled. "Yes, it's wonderful," she said finally. There were no noises at all coming through the baby monitor except the gentle, even sounds of a child breathing.

Lisa was stretched out on Max and Deborah's sofa. Carole sat nearby, draped sideways across an oversized, overstuffed chair. Carole's attention was focused on the book she held, which was about the benefits of longeing horses. Lisa was reading *The Black Stallion* for the fourteenth time. The girls felt completely content and relaxed—now that Maxi was asleep.

Their offer to help look after Maxi hadn't originally included evening baby-sitting, but both Deborah and Max had been working so hard that the girls thought they needed a night out together without Maxi in tow, so they'd told the tired parents to go have some fun. Besides, it gave them a chance to pick really good books from Max's library.

Lisa set her book down. "You know, I think I feel a little sorry for Stevie."

"Because she hasn't had a chance to run after Maxi for three whole days?" Carole asked.

"No, because she's probably being dragged around to a whole bunch of boring museums, and there are so few horses anywhere in the city."

"You know that if there are horses, Stevie will find them," said Carole.

"Well, sure, it's sort of a Saddle Club thing, isn't it? We're horse magnets. But it's not always easy and we don't know whether the girl she's staying with rides. I mean, Stevie must be bored out of her mind, don't you think?"

"It seems to me that Stevie has a talent for making

things happen. My sixth sense tells me she's not bored at all."

"You're probably right," Lisa conceded. "And she's probably teaching that girl—what's her name, Regina?—a thing or two about getting into trouble!"

"HELLO?" A VOICE whispered through the darkness.

Nobody said anything.

"You guys!" the voice said. "I'm sure I heard you. Are you there?"

It was Liza! It wasn't police, robbers, muggers, murderers, or worse. It was Liza. Stevie let out a huge sigh of relief.

"Get in here!" Regina said sharply. "Don't let anybody see you."

"Nobody can see anything down here," Liza said, climbing through the window and down the tower of boxes. "It's completely dark. Did they turn off the electricity?"

"What are you doing here?" Stevie asked. The one thing that had made sense to her all evening was that Liza had had the presence of mind to stay home. She couldn't imagine what had made her decide to come.

"I told Ann I'd be here, but I had to go someplace with my mother. Didn't she tell you?"

"Uh, sort of," Regina said. That seemed to Stevie as good an answer as any.

"So, ghost stories? Are we going to tell them or what?" Liza asked.

Regina shrugged. She handed the stethoscope back to Peter. "This doesn't work at all," she said. "We're never going to find out what's in here, so we might as well go back upstairs."

The whole crew trooped back up the basement stairs and then up again to the parlor floor. Peter and Ann re-lit the candles and the group settled themselves back on the boxes they'd put around the fireplace.

"Now, where were we?" Regina asked. "I remember. It was something about thirteen candles. . . ." She looked at Stevie expectantly.

Stevie remembered, too. She knew the story perfectly well. She'd told it many times. It was a campfire favorite of The Saddle Club. Even her boyfriend, Phil, and his friend A.J. shivered when she told it. It *was* a very scary story. Somehow, though, tonight it didn't seem very scary. It wasn't anywhere near as frightening as having Frank and Maurice arrive in the middle of their game. It wasn't even as scary as having Liza show up at the basement window when they'd thought they were alone. Stevie was beginning to consider the possibility of giving up telling ghost stories altogether. She thought she'd had enough of a scare for one night.

"Come on, Stevie, tell it!" Regina urged her.

"I think I've forgotten what I was going to say. Why doesn't someone else tell a story?" she suggested.

Gordon tried. He told one about a monster that hid in the woods. Stevie had heard lots of variations of it. The only way it worked was if the storyteller set up the fact that when the monster is on the loose, a bell rings or a siren sounds. Gordon didn't realize that, and it wasn't scary at all the way he told it. Stevie thought that maybe his heart wasn't in it. Maybe, like Stevie, he wasn't interested in being scared anymore. Maybe, being younger than the rest of them, he was already too scared to think very clearly—although Stevie thought maybe they were all feeling that way, no matter how old they were.

Peter looked at his watch. "Isn't it time to go home?" he asked. Those were the words Stevie had been waiting to hear ever since they'd gotten there!

"Yeah," said Gordon. "Come on."

He stood up. He was tired, and when people get

tired, they sometimes get clumsy, especially when they are little kids, which is exactly what Gordon was. He kicked the candle in front of him. He obviously didn't mean to do it. Nobody ever thought it was intentional and nobody ever thought Gordon had any idea what would happen as a consequence.

The floor was covered with dust and sawdust and construction debris. The candle flame caught onto a curl of dry wood that had settled next to a small paper bag that was next to a small pile of sawdust. Only it all happened in a second. Maybe less than that.

Suddenly a whole section of the floor was on fire.

"Step on it!" Stevie called out. She and her friends began stomping on the flames as fast and as hard as they could, chasing them wherever they caught.

The flames raced like water running downhill, in three directions at once, toward the windows, the fireplace, and then the stairs to the ground floor—the kids' only means of escape. The fire fueled itself on litter scattered all over the floor that the kids had barely noticed until it exploded into flames.

"We've got to get this out!" yelled Stevie.

"There it goes over there!" said Peter, racing after the line of fire that was stretching toward the stack of boxes. They had no idea what was in those boxes. A construction site could contain sand and gravel that couldn't burn or paint thinner that could explode.

Regina pulled off her jacket and began using it to swat at the flames. Ann did the same. It helped until the flames headed for the back room, where there were stacks of lumber, apparently to be used for the new stairs up to the third floor from the parlor. Everybody knew that wood burns well. Especially wood that's just been varnished!

STEVIE SLAPPED AT the last lick of flame while Peter stepped on the final embers.

"And we thought the worst thing that could happen was if those guys came back!" Stevie joked.

The rest of the group laughed but not very hard. There was nothing funny about fire, and they'd just had a very close call.

"I never saw anything catch fire so fast!" said Liza.

"It was like an explosion," Peter said.

"It's because the place is so dirty," Regina told them. "The only way it gets worse is if there's dust in the air that catches on fire."

"That happens in stables sometimes," said Stevie. "The

83

air can be filled with dust from the hay, straw, and feed grains, so the old wood that most stables are made of isn't the only danger: The air itself becomes an explosive."

"Fortunately this place wasn't that messy," said Ann.

"No, but I've just decided that when I get back to Virginia, I'm going to reconsider cleaning up my room!" said Stevie.

"And speaking of getting home . . . ," said Peter, taking Gordon's hand.

"Yes, go," said Regina. "The fire seems to be completely out, but"—she glanced at her watch—"Stevie and I have another fifteen minutes until our curfew. I think someone should stick around to be absolutely sure. Fire can kind of hide for a while."

"I think that's a good idea, and we'll go on one condition," said Peter.

"Yes?" Stevie asked, wondering why anybody would put any conditions on that at all.

"If it breaks out again, you guys run out of here as fast as you can and call the fire department. There's no way two of you alone could put out another fire like the one we just saw."

"Deal," said Stevie before Regina could have another bright idea.

A few seconds later Stevie and Regina were alone in the house. The two of them examined the remains of the fire in the parlor. Oddly, because what had burned were scraps and dust, Stevie couldn't find any damage to the building. There were just loads of cinders and charred trash scattered across the floor.

"Boy, were we lucky," said Regina.

Stevie didn't think *lucky* was the right word. *Stupid* came closer. But then again, she knew they had been lucky. The fire could have been much worse.

"I don't see anything here that looks like it's still dangerous," said Regina. "Even when I touch the stuff, it feels cold by now. That means we can go, I guess."

"I guess," said Stevie. Those were the nicest words she'd heard in a long time! They picked up the remainders of everything the kids had brought with them. Stevie put six candles and lots of snack food, including the big bag of raisins, into Regina's backpack. She took a last look. It was messy, but she was pretty certain the fire was out and they could go.

The two girls hurried down the stairs, following their friends by only a few minutes. On the ground floor they turned the corner to the basement stairs, passing by a closed door on their way.

"That's the kitchen in there, isn't it?" Stevie asked.

"I guess. We've never been in there."

"I wonder if we could find a kitchen bucket," said Stevie. "And if the water is running, which I think it must be, then we could take a bucket of water upstairs and slosh it across the floor."

"But if we do that, the men will know for sure that we've been here and they'll lock up everything! We'll never get back in."

Stevie couldn't believe her ears. After all that had happened tonight, Regina was worried about hiding their tracks and being able to come back?

"Are you nuts?" Stevie asked, trying to contain herself.

"That *was* really stupid, wasn't it?" Regina asked.

Stevie didn't answer her. She pulled open the door to the old kitchen and shone her flashlight around. It definitely had been the kitchen. There was a place where a stove had been, and there were a refrigerator and cabinets and a sink. Stevie stepped over to the sink and turned on the tap. Water came spouting out as if nothing had ever gone wrong in the place. Stevie laughed.

"It works," she declared. "Now all we need is a bucket—or something else to carry the water in."

The kitchen was scattered with reminders of its prior tenants, as well as of the slow-moving construction project. The sink's drain board had become the resting place for two paper cups half filled with coffee. They didn't seem like a practical way to wet the whole floor upstairs.

Regina pulled open some cabinets near the sink and played her flashlight across them. Nothing. Underneath the sink they found some cleaning products, apparently considered unworthy of moving. Closer examination revealed evidence of mice as previous occupants.

"Let's just close that up," she suggested, wrinkling her nose in distaste.

Stevie put her hands on her hips and looked around. "There must be something."

"We don't really have to do this, Stevie," Regina said. "I'm pretty sure the fire's out."

"We're trespassing on someone else's property," Stevie reminded her. "We started a fire here and we didn't want to call the fire department. I think we need to be one hundred percent sure it's out."

Stevie looked around, shining her flashlight into

the corner, trying to be sure she knew what everything was and hoping she'd see something that would carry water. On the other wall were signs of the former presence of a washing machine and dryer: water spigots and an exhaust hose. Next to those was a tall cabinet.

"Broom closet!" Stevie said. Her mother always kept a bucket in the broom closet, because that's where the mop was. If these people had left cleaning supplies under the sink, maybe they'd left a bucket.

She stepped across the kitchen and reached for the broom closet door. She pulled it open and ran the flashlight around in it. When she looked down, she saw something that astonished her.

"Regina! Come look at this!" said Stevie, gesturing with the flashlight.

"What is it?"

"Come see!" Stevie replied.

Regina hurried over and looked where Stevie was pointing. Her jaw dropped.

"Oh, isn't it just like you to find—" she began. "What's that?"

Stevie felt a trembling beneath her feet. She reached out to grab Regina, who was already clutching her. In a split second she realized that the best thing to do wasn't to get closer to Regina but farther away. The combined weight of the two girls had stressed the old floor beyond its capacity. The floorboards were crumbling!

There was a horrible wrenching sound, a creak, and a snap, all within seconds of one another, and then the floor beneath them gave way.

"Aaaaaah!" Regina screamed.

"Uuuuurrgh!" yowled Stevie.

The two girls fell.

It seemed like they were in the air for an eternity. The girls clutched at each other on their downward journey. It didn't, in fact, take very long. It just seemed that way.

They landed in the basement, accompanied by the remains of some very weak floorboards and a fair amount of dust, which continued tumbling down for a while, landing on their heads and all around them.

Stevie still held a flashlight in her hand, but it had turned off when she'd squeezed it in fright. She pushed the button to turn it back on. Obediently, a beam of light appeared.

The girls looked around, orienting themselves.

They were in the basement, all right. That was the only place to go from the ground floor. But they were in a part of the basement they'd never seen before.

Stevie moved the light around to be sure she was seeing right, and then she knew she was. "Uh-oh . . ."

"Oh no," said Regina.

They were in a small cramped room that was filled with stacks of boxes. Two walls were the familiar walls of the basement, constructed of rough concrete. Two others were clearly new plywood. They were inside the mysterious locked closet.

"And to think this was so easy to get into all the time!" Stevie joked feebly.

"Getting in was one thing," said Regina.

Stevie looked at the room again, absorbing the implications of what Regina had just said. The room *was* locked. Totally, utterly locked. The way they'd gotten in was above them—way above them. They couldn't reach the ceiling, and even if they could, the whole floor above was so weak, they probably couldn't get out.

Stevie sank down onto a box.

"What are you thinking?" Regina asked, clearly hoping it would be the answer to their most urgent question.

"You know what they say," Stevie said.

"No, what?"

" 'Be careful what you wish for. You might just get it.' "

Regina sat down on the box next to her with a sigh.

9

"WE'RE STUCK," SAID Regina.

"For good," said Stevie.

They sat glumly on their boxes, elbows on their knees and chins on their hands.

"Did you get hurt?" Stevie asked.

"I think just a scrape," said Regina. "You?"

"Same," said Stevie. "Well, maybe a bruise, too." She rubbed her sore bottom and pointed her flashlight up at the ceiling. The beam of light above her showed how far they'd traveled. "I guess we're lucky."

"Some luck," said Regina.

Stevie didn't have a response to that. She used the flashlight to scan the room again. Maybe the secret closet held another secret, like a way out.

No such thing. It did, however, have a switch on the wall.

She flipped the switch and a fluorescent light flickered on.

"That's better," Stevie said, turning off her flashlight.

She sat down again.

"I wonder how long we can survive down here without food and water," Regina said.

Stevie thought the comment was a mark of just how upset Regina was. "First of all, we are not without food and water," she said. "You've got the backpack with all our goodies in it, right?"

"Okay, so how long can we survive on"—she burrowed in the backpack—"chocolate milk, marshmallows, cheese crackers, raisins, and diet soda?"

"Sounds like the major food groups to me!" quipped Stevie. Even to her, the joke sounded weak. "But anyway, the other thing is that it can't take too long before someone notices we're gone. Morning at the latest, I'd say. Our moms are going to freak out."

"I'll be grounded until I'm twenty-five," said Regina.

"Me too," said Stevie. "If my parents don't completely disown me first."

Their prospects were grim. Stevie had known from the very start that what they were doing was wrong. Breaking into someone else's house was considered against the law everywhere in the civilized world. New York City was not going to be an exception. If it hadn't been for Regina . . .

"Maybe we can escape first," said Regina.

"We're going to need wings to do it," said Stevie, glancing back up at the ceiling.

"If only you hadn't had the bright idea of putting water on the floor to douse the fire."

"Me? You think this is *my* fault?" Stevie asked.

"Well, what got us down here?" said Regina.

"It isn't what got us down here that's the problem," said Stevie. "It was coming to this house in the first place. I mean, once those guys started nailing us inside this afternoon, you might have taken the hint that we shouldn't be here."

"I didn't exactly have to talk you into it," said Regina.

"I came because I wanted to be sure you wouldn't get into any trouble!" said Stevie.

"And a swell job you did of that," Regina retorted.

It was going to take Stevie a few minutes to think of a good answer to that one. She shifted her weight on the box where she sat and tried to think of a bright side to their predicament. It was a challenge.

"And if you weren't such a goody-goody, we could have left with the other guys!" Regina blurted out.

It took a moment for the words to sink in. Stevie had never, ever, in her whole life been called a goody-goody. Miserable as their situation was—scraped, bruised, humiliated, facing a lifetime of being grounded, subject to starvation (except for marshmallows and raisins)—there was something totally bizarre about Regina referring to her as a goody-goody. She tried to stifle her reaction, but there was no way around it. She started laughing and couldn't stop. Regina joined in. The two of them sat in the stuffy closet, with the dust still settling from the broken ceiling above, laughing as hard as they ever had.

95

Stevie wiped away some tears. Regina snorted, and they both laughed again until they were exhausted. Then they just sat, each contemplating their considerable predicament.

"I guess I kind of liked the idea of being sure the fire was out," Regina conceded, handing Stevie a cracker.

"And I kind of liked the idea of wowing you and your friends with my cool ghost stories," said Stevie.

"Quite a pair, aren't we?" Regina asked.

"I think maybe it's a good thing we didn't meet until now. We'd already be grounded for life, and I would hate to have missed this! I just wish Lisa and Carole were here. They'd know what to do."

"They would have known better than to get into this situation—from what you tell me."

"You know, we spent a lot of time trying to figure out how to get into this room," said Stevie.

"Why didn't we think of the magnificent collapsing floor entry before?" teased Regina.

"Too easy," said Stevie. "Anyway, I'm still wondering why this place is locked so tight. Since we're here, we ought to take a look at what's inside these boxes."

Regina stood up and looked at the box she'd been sitting on. It was a simple dark brown carton with a lift-off lid, the kind her mother used for storing papers.

She removed the lid and looked inside.

"Paper," she said.

"Like for a printer?" asked Stevie, peering in.

"No, used paper," said Regina. "Stuff that's already been through a printer. Files."

Stevie crouched and looked for herself. Regina was right. The entire box was filled with all kinds of papers, clipped and stapled together. Most of it looked like receipts for things and lists of supplies that had been ordered and delivered.

"Drywall," Stevie read, looking at one of the receipts.

"What's that?"

"The stuff they use to make walls, like to divide a big room into smaller ones," said Stevie. She knew about it because the contractors had used drywall when they'd redone the Lakes' kitchen. She looked at the receipt again. "A lot of drywall," she said.

"I guess you need a lot of drywall when you're renovating a house like this."

"Not really," said Stevie. "I think they build houses differently now from the way they did. All these walls are plaster. They wouldn't replace them with drywall."

She picked up another receipt. "Four hundred thousand tiles," she read.

"For the bathroom?" Regina asked.

"Only if it's the bathroom in Grand Central Station," said Stevie. "That's almost half a million tiles. If they were going to tile this entire house, maybe—and on the outside, too."

"Doesn't seem likely."

"This guy must be working on a lot of places at the same time," Stevie reasoned.

"Maybe," said Regina.

Stevie noticed then that there were filing cabinets around them. She pulled open a drawer. More paper. And the one next to it. More paper.

"Weird," said Stevie.

Regina agreed.

"This is one busy contractor," said Stevie. Then she pulled open the next drawer. The only thing in it was a notebook. Stevie picked it up to look inside, but there was a lock on it. She started thinking about what kind of information needed to be kept in a locked notebook in a locked room in an empty house. It all seemed very odd and, she decided again, none of her business. She wished she'd never wondered about it at all.

"This is so dumb!" said Regina. "Boring, I mean. I wish we'd never even thought of looking in here."

"Me too," said Stevie, knowing she meant that very sincerely.

Stevie had the weird sensation that between her and Regina, she was the one with some common sense and she was going to need to draw on it to get them out of the house in one piece. She thought about Carole and Lisa. Although they weren't there, there seemed to be ways they were always with her. So, what would Carole do? The answer was obvious. Carole would find a way to get a horse to rescue them. That seemed highly unlikely. Lisa, on the other hand, would very sensibly say that the thing to do was relax. They would be rescued.

"So, what have we got with us?" Stevie asked, eyeing the backpack.

Regina rummaged again and handed Stevie the bag of raisins and a warm can of diet soda. It didn't look like much of a meal, but Stevie opened the raisin bag and chewed on a couple pieces of the dried fruit.

"What else?"

Regina stuck her hand in again. "I've still got the stethoscope," she said. "It didn't do us much good on the other side of the wall; I don't know that it'll be helpful in here."

"Probably not, but we can listen to each other's hearts. Let me have that a second."

Stevie stuck the earpieces in her ear and held the other end to her own heart. It was beating, all right. She thought it was probably beating faster than it usually did, and it had already had quite a workout that night.

Listening to her heart beat was not going to be a full-time occupation. She stood up and put the stethoscope against the wooden wall above a filing cabinet. There were no sounds at all at first, and then she thought she heard a sort of scurrying sound. She definitely did *not* want to know what that was.

She took the stethoscope over to the concrete wall she knew was part of the front of the house, facing the street. There she could hear lots of sounds.

"Water running," she said.

"Could be a water main or a sewer," Regina suggested.

Stevie hoped it was a water main. "There's a subway!" she said. She pulled the earpieces out of her ears and could hear nothing. Back against the wall with the stethoscope, it was clear as could be.

"It's just a block from here. Sometimes I notice it late at night," Regina confirmed.

"Well, it's definitely there," Stevie said.

She listened some more. She could hear people walking by out on the street. There was the sure and sharp clicking of a woman's high heels. Stevie wondered where she'd been that night. Theater, dance? Maybe a fancy restaurant? Not that it mattered, but it was something to think about.

Then there was another sound, something she never expected to hear.

"Hooves!" she declared. "It's a horse!"

"Give me a break," said Regina.

"No, for real," said Stevie, offering the stethoscope to Regina, who took it and listened.

"Clip-clop, definitely a horse," she said.

"Who would go for a ride at this hour and in this place?" Stevie asked.

"It must be a police horse," said Regina. "There is a stable here—"

"Yeah, but it's way over on the West Side," said Stevie. If there was one thing she knew about New York City, it was where she could find a stable. "And I doubt they let riders go out at night."

"So it's definitely a police horse," said Regina.

"Just what we need!" Stevie told her. Then she turned toward the wall they'd been listening to and cried, "Help!" She put the stethoscope to the wall again to see if there was any response. Nothing. *"Help!"* she screamed louder. Again, no response. "Come on, help me here," she said to Regina, who was looking at her very doubtfully. Regina shrugged. Together the two of them screamed as loud as they could: *"HELP!"* Then they listened again, Stevie with the stethoscope, Regina with her ear pressed against the wall. The only sound they heard was the sound of hoofbeats receding.

Stevie shook her head. For just a few minutes she'd been sure that the Carole system of rescue was going to work—that there would be a horse to come to their aid. But that wasn't happening.

She listened some more at the wall. If the policeman hadn't been able to hear them, it was very doubtful that anybody else would. It turned out not to make a difference, though. There were no other sounds from outside. Stevie glanced at her watch. It was nearly midnight. Nobody was out on the street in the city that never sleeps.

And then there *was* another sound. It was the clip-clop of horseshoes on asphalt again. Only this time there were more clips and clops.

"Two horses," Stevie told Regina, who just looked at her in disbelief.

"Some tracker you are," said Regina. "I bet you can tell whether they're left- or right-handed from the way the clips and clops come down the street."

"Of course not," said Stevie. "Horses aren't 'handed' the way people are."

"I wouldn't have known that," said Regina, but she clearly wasn't impressed. In fact, she seemed irritated. "It's not that you're horse-crazy that bothers me," she said. "It's that you're horse-silly."

"Little do you know," said Stevie, trying to keep the irritation out of her own voice. It wasn't going to do any good to get into another argument at this point. And besides, the policemen and their horses didn't seem to be coming to their rescue any better in twos than singly.

103

When she could no longer hear the hoofbeats, Stevie took off the stethoscope and sat down again on one of the boxes of paper. She leaned back, resting her head against a filing cabinet. She closed her eyes and drifted into an uneasy sleep.

CAROLE SAT BOLT upright in bed. Something was chasing around in her mind. She glanced at the clock. It read 2:13 A.M. She squeezed her eyes shut in an attempt to clear her mind a little. What was it that was chasing around?

Maxi. No, it wasn't Maxi chasing around, it was Carole chasing Maxi around. As she settled back onto her pillow, she remembered the day she and Lisa had had with Maxi. She sighed. They just had a few more days of Maxi chasing and then she'd be able to rest.

It would be easier if Stevie were here, Carole thought. Stevie always seemed to find ways to make the toughest chore more fun. She'd have thought of all sorts of clever and fun things to do with Maxi. It might not have made the work any easier, but it would have made it more enjoyable.

Things were always more fun when Stevie was around.

Stevie was in New York, though, probably having the time of her life. Carole and Lisa would get a whole bunch of postcards from all the great places she'd been in the city. The postcards would arrive long after Stevie got home and had a chance to tell them all the fun stories about her trip. And all they'd have to tell her was how fast Maxi had run into which stall at which time. They could tell her how much Maxi loved to ride the ponies. Stevie would like that. It wouldn't surprise her, but she'd like it.

Carole's eyes drifted closed again. It was silly to think about what Stevie was doing at that moment, because it was obvious that she'd be sleeping. Anybody with any sense would be sleeping at 2:13 in the morning, even in New York where there were so many street noises it must be impossible to sleep. Yes, even Stevie would be asleep then.

Carole's last thought before she fell back to sleep was of Stevie standing on the top of the Empire State Building, waving at her.

"STEVIE!" A WHISPERING voice penetrated Stevie's sleep.

"Wha—"

"Stevie!"

Her eyes fluttered open.

"Did you hear that?"

The only thing she'd heard was Regina's voice. She shook her head.

"Listen!"

They sat quietly, waiting, listening.

Stevie looked at her watch. It was almost a quarter past two. Who was still awake at that hour? And why?

It occurred to Stevie that perhaps the only thing worse than having her mother find out what she'd been up to would be if those men came back and discovered two girls in their secret room. The secret of it was still a mystery, since the only thing they'd found was paper, but the fact that those men didn't want anyone in the house had come through clear as a bell.

She stood up and flicked the light off. It wouldn't exactly hide them from those guys, but then it wouldn't advertise their presence, either. As long as the men didn't go into the kitchen, where they would come across a large and rather suggestive hole in the floor . . .

"I guess that won't make much difference," said Stevie, sitting back down. Regina shrugged. It didn't hurt, either—at least until they'd found out what that noise was. Regina took Stevie's hand and held it tight. They were in this together.

There was a distinct shuffling in the basement. Then a thump, followed by a *shush!*

And another thump, and another.

Stevie pressed her ear to the door, but all the sounds were muffled. Then she remembered the stethoscope. She slipped that into her ears and tried listening again.

At first all she could discern were footsteps. There was a click that sounded like a light being turned on. She grimaced, looking at Regina. What if it was the two men again? The next thing they would hear would be the sounds of keys going into the locks. How would they ever explain? How could they ever get away?

Stevie held her breath. What she heard next was not a key going into a lock. It was the distinct sound of a sneaker hitting the bottom step of the staircase up to the ground floor.

"Be quiet!" one voice said. It was a familiar voice. It wasn't gruff and it wasn't threatening.

"Our moms are going to kill us!" said another voice.

"Well, they've got to be here someplace and we have to find them!" said the first.

Liza and Peter. That's who was speaking.

"Shhhhh!" Stevie suspected that was Ann.

Stevie knocked on the door.

"Hey, guys!" she said.

"Is that you?" Peter asked.

"Who were you expecting?" Regina snapped back. "Of course it's us. Get us out of here!"

"How'd you get in there?"

"There's a slight weakness in the kitchen floor," Stevie said.

"We fell," Regina explained.

"Are you okay?" Ann asked.

"We will be as soon as you get us out of here!" said Regina.

"Well, how are we supposed to do that?" Liza asked.

"How should I know?" said Regina. "You're the ones in charge of rescuing!"

It was funny and it made Stevie smile, but it didn't solve the problem. She had an idea, though. "I think I saw a ladder upstairs," she told them. "In the parlor, by the stairs going up to the next floor."

"Well, how are we going to get it to you?" Liza asked.

"Through the ceiling!" Regina snapped. She was clearly annoyed with the rescuers' inability to rescue them.

Stevie knew that they'd figure it out and that the most difficult part was going to be walking on the kitchen floor with the ladder. If it collapsed with the two girls there alone, how would it behave with more kids and a ladder?

Stevie took a deep breath and thought of what Lisa would do. Logically, she understood that the weak floor was a problem, that Peter, Ann, and Liza would know it was a problem, and that they would solve it.

They did.

A few minutes later Peter had laid the ladder across the weakened kitchen floor and was crawling along it to the edge of the hole, testing the strength of the floor as he went. When he neared the hole the girls had fallen through a mere four hours earlier, he was especially cautious. He obviously knew he had to be sure that the floor would hold him, the ladder, and one of the girls. Fortunately there was a beam right there. He could stand securely on the part of the floor right over the beam. Carefully he lifted the long wooden ladder and slid it down into the room where Stevie and Regina were trapped.

One at a time, the girls climbed up the ladder and then walked along the floor over the beam to the safety of the dining room, where they found Liza and Ann waiting for them with hugs.

Peter left the ladder in the hole. There was no point in bothering to pretend they hadn't been there.

Stevie found herself overwhelmed with relief as she stood embracing her rescuers. She'd really thought they were going to be in there a lot longer and that their rescuers were going to be much more angry than relieved.

"How did you know we were stuck?" Stevie said.

"Regina's mother called," said Ann.

"Oh, she must be going out of her gourd!" said Regina.

"Give us some credit," said Ann. "She thinks you're sleeping over at our place."

"How'd you swing that?" Stevie asked.

"When you didn't show up at ten, I guess your mom got worried. It was about eleven when she called. Our mother answered the phone. She knew a bunch of us had come in earlier, including Liza, and I think she just figured we were all together. I heard her on the phone. It was perfect. 'Oh, no problem,' she said. 'The kids are all upstairs. They're so quiet, they must be asleep. I'll send them home in the morning.' And that was it."

"Mom didn't want to bawl me out?" Regina asked.

"I guess not. I guess she figured as long as you guys were at our house, it was okay."

"But you knew we weren't," Stevie said.

"Right. And we also knew you wouldn't want your mother or anyone else to know that."

"Weren't you worried about us?" Regina asked. Stevie thought she must be wondering the same thing she was: Why had it taken them so long to come to the rescue?

"Of course we were," said Ann. "Like crazy. But we couldn't come over here until our parents were asleep. We sort of figured you two had gotten back to ghost stories and lost track of the time."

"For four hours?" Regina asked.

Liza shrugged. "We're here now. You're safe. Want to complain about something else?"

"Thanks for coming back to get us," Stevie said.

"No problem," said Liza. "We were glad to be of service, at risk of life and limb—"

"Lots of problems, actually," said Stevie. "So thanks. Say, does anybody want to get a good night's sleep?"

She didn't have to ask the question twice. As fast as they could, the five kids all returned to the basement, squeezed back through the window, and began the journey home. Stevie was the last one out. She looked behind her into the darkness, realizing they'd left the light on in the secret room. It didn't matter. The contractor would certainly know that someone had been there. She didn't think he'd ever be able to figure out who it was. She whispered good-bye into the shadows behind her. If there was one thing of which she was certain, it was that she would never return to that house again. Ever.

11

MAXI WAS CRYING and Stevie could hear her. She wasn't far away, but she wasn't close, either. The sound she made was a long moaning wail that cut into the night. It faded for a second and then came back, louder, more insistent.

"I'm coming!" Stevie called back, trying to reassure the child. Where was Carole? Where was Lisa? She had no idea. She was only aware of herself and the crying child. She couldn't find Maxi. All she could do was hear her.

She reached out in the darkness. Her hand hit something. It was a lamp and it crashed loudly to the floor.

"What's that?"

Stevie squinted in the dim light and realized it was Regina who had spoken.

"Someone was crying," Stevie said, now sitting up in bed.

"What? I don't hear any crying. What time is it? What's going on?"

Stevie could only answer one of those questions, so she did. "It's three-oh-four," she said. She reached over and picked up the bedside lamp she'd so unceremoniously knocked to the floor. She tried the switch. It turned on. "What's that sound?" she asked.

"Oh, that," said Regina. "It's a siren."

Of course it was a siren. They had sirens in Willow Creek. Stevie heard them occasionally, but usually not late at night and never so close—except for the time the Ziegler twins had decided to have a barbecue in their fireplace without opening the flue. That had been pretty big excitement on the street where Stevie lived. But it had happened in the middle of a Saturday afternoon, not at 3:04 in the morning.

Regina lay back down on the pillow. She closed her eyes. "Let's go back to sleep," she said.

It seemed like an awfully good idea. They hadn't

been in bed very long at all. As soon as they'd left the old house, the kids had scurried back to their own homes and gotten into bed as fast as possible. Both girls were grateful that the garden door to the Evanses' house had been unlocked. Otherwise they would've had to climb the fire escape to Regina's window on the third floor, and frankly they'd had enough adventure for one night.

Now, though, there seemed to be more adventure going on. The sirens were getting louder and more insistent.

"They're stopping!" said Regina.

"That's good," said Stevie.

"No it isn't," Regina replied.

"Why not?" Stevie asked. Although there were sirens in Willow Creek, they were much more common in New York, and Stevie recognized that Regina was going to be more of an expert on them than she was, especially in her sleepy state.

Regina explained patiently. "What you want with sirens is to have them fade away as the emergency vehicles pass by. These just got louder and stopped. Whatever they're doing, it's nearby. In fact, it's on this block. C'mon."

She slipped out of bed, grabbed a bathrobe, and slid

her feet into slippers. Stevie followed her into the hall.

They went down a flight of stairs into the front room on the second floor. They pulled the curtains aside and lifted the shades. The whole street, narrow to begin with, was filled with police cars and emergency vehicles. There was a fire department rescue truck and two ambulances. All of them were clustered at the end of the block, right next to the building that had so recently been Stevie and Regina's prison.

Stevie's voice stuck in her throat before she could ask the question that Regina sputtered out.

"Did—Did the fire come back?"

The girls opened the window as wide as they could and hung out to get a better look. One glance answered that question. There were no fire trucks, just other emergency vehicles. Whatever the problem was, it wasn't fire.

Stevie thought about sighing with relief, but the fact that the place was filled with emergency vehicles right after they'd been stuck in it suggested to her that perhaps all this activity might have something to do with them.

"What's going on, girls?"

It was Mrs. Evans, standing behind them, also wearing her bathrobe and slippers.

"Beats me," said Regina.

Stevie thought that was a good answer.

"Elisa?" Stevie recognized her own mother's voice. "Oh, Stevie," her mother said. "Well, good morning, ladies. Some wake-up system you have in this city!"

The mothers laughed. Stevie and Regina weren't quite so sure a laugh was in order.

"Gee, what are you girls doing here?" Mrs. Evans asked. "I thought you were over at Peter's house."

In the confusion of the escape and their overwhelming desire to be someplace safe and familiar, both girls had completely forgotten that Peter's mother had told Mrs. Evans they were staying over there. Regina, ever fast on her feet, came up with an answer. "Stevie got homesick," she said.

That earned Stevie a strange look from her mother, who knew perfectly well that Stevie never got homesick, but there was so much else going on at that moment that she didn't inquire any further. Stevie hoped she never would.

"Well, come on," said Mrs. Evans, mercifully changing the subject. "We're not going to learn anything standing here. Let's join the rest of our neighbors on the street and see what's really going on."

For the first time Stevie noticed that a crowd was collecting on the corner. She smiled as she watched them. There was a large cluster of people, most of them in pajamas and bathrobes, some in quickly assembled outfits, all trying to determine what was going on.

Mrs. Evans tucked a set of house keys into her bathrobe pocket and led the way down the stairs and out into the street.

If a lot of that evening had already been surreal to Stevie, standing out on the street that night might have been the most surreal. Nobody had any idea what was going on, but Stevie and Regina, who did have an idea of what was going on, were most confused of all. Or at least Stevie suspected they had an idea.

"Do you think we set off some kind of alarm?" Regina asked.

"Probably not," said Stevie. "If there was an alarm system, we would have tripped it ages ago—like the first time we were in there."

"Okay, so what's going on?"

"The contractor came back and saw that the place had been broken into?" Stevie suggested. That seemed like a very real possibility.

"At three o'clock in the morning?" Regina asked.

Maybe it wasn't such a real possibility after all.

Nearby, Mrs. Evans was greeting neighbors. The big question on everybody's lips was "What's going on?"

"I heard there was a homeless person living in there," one person said. "Maybe they're just evicting him."

"At three o'clock in the morning?" Regina whispered to Stevie. They exchanged smiles.

"Oh, no," said another neighbor. "It's the Perseys—they're the ones who own the place. I think they're moving in this week."

"At three o'clock in the morning?" Stevie whispered to Regina.

It was funny that the two of them had some pretty dumb ideas about what was going on, but it seemed the adults' ideas were even dumber!

"It must be bad, whatever it is," said another neighbor. "Otherwise we wouldn't need all these rescue trucks."

That made sense.

By the time Stevie, Regina, and their mothers had arrived on the scene, all the emergency vehicles were parked and empty, so it was clear that the emergency rescue people had already gone in. They began coming out, emptyhanded.

"I guess there's nobody to rescue," Stevie observed quietly.

"We already knew that," said Regina.

But the trucks didn't leave. In fact, more police cars and detectives arrived. And then a large van pulled up and four men went into the house. They were in there a long time.

"I guess they found a body," said the neighbor who had been convinced the Perseys were moving in that night.

Stevie was sure he was wrong. If there had been a body, they'd have had a medical examiner's truck instead of the big van they'd brought. She was even surer there wasn't a body when the van group returned and took a couple of dollies and handcarts back in with them.

"What are those for?" Regina asked.

"They use them to carry heavy things," Stevie explained. "You see moving men with those."

"Oh, right," said Regina.

"Stevie," said her mother. "Isn't this exciting? There's always something going on in New York!"

Stevie nodded in agreement, but she wasn't so sure. She was afraid this "excitement" was going to have some repercussions, and she was already thinking about what it was going to be like to be grounded for a year.

For a long time nothing happened. Nobody moved from the street, and nobody came out of the house. The neighbors waited with anticipation.

Then things started happening very quickly. The van crew began emerging from the house, their dollies and handcarts loaded down with filing cabinets. Each cabinet had wide yellow tape around it, stating POLICE EVIDENCE: DO NOT TAMPER.

"That's not evidence," Stevie grumbled. "Those are just filing cabinets!"

"The same ones we were sitting on a couple of hours ago," said Regina.

Stevie was pretty sure Regina was right about that, though she couldn't tell the difference between one filing cabinet and another. On the other hand, she was quite certain there hadn't been any other filing cabinets in the house.

Then, just in time to reassure Stevie that they were, in fact, the same filing cabinets, an officer came out carrying a backpack, a container of chocolate milk, some cheese crackers, and a large bag of raisins.

"Toast," Regina said.

The very word Stevie was going to use.

"Hi, guys. How's it going?" It was Peter. He was there with the rest of his family. They were all in their bathrobes, too.

"Did you see that?" Regina asked, pointing to her backpack and its contents, now safely in the hands of the law.

"How could you forget it?" Peter asked.

"I wasn't thinking of evidence," said Regina. "I was just thinking about getting out of there!"

"Maybe I should have thought of it," said Stevie.

"No, it's my bag," Regina said.

"Well, the police don't know that," said Peter. "How could they find out?"

"DNA evidence on the raisins," Stevie said.

"I suppose, or maybe fingerprints," said Peter.

"How about my name tag?" said Regina. "It'll save them a lot of lab work if they just read it."

"You are so busted!" said Peter.

"Will you visit me in jail?" Regina asked.

"Visit you? We'll be in adjoining cells!"

"Oh, hi, Peter," said Mrs. Evans. "Pretty exciting, isn't it?"

"It sure is, Mrs. Evans. But I guess we'll probably never really know everything that's going on here, will we?"

Stevie wished he weren't trying to be so helpful. It wasn't helping, she was sure.

"I would think we would," said Mrs. Evans, correcting him. "I mean, this is our neighborhood. We'll find out."

That was just what Stevie and Regina were dreading.

Pretty soon the police began packing up their cars. They put up some yellow tape, declaring the house to be a crime scene and forbidding anyone from going inside. Stevie and Regina knew they would have no trouble following that rule!

"Looks like the excitement is over," said Mrs. Lake. "Let's finish up that good night's sleep."

Stevie followed her mother and Mrs. Evans back to the house, the two girls lagging behind the women by a few feet just in case there was anything they needed to discuss. There wasn't, really. Both girls knew that in spite of Mrs. Lake's enthusiasm about a good night's sleep, it was going to be very hard for them to go back to bed. They both knew they hadn't heard the end of the exciting activities of the night.

"Maybe we'd better try to sleep," said Regina.

"Yeah, it's going to be our last night of freedom, and we should enjoy it," said Stevie. "I think the other shoe is going to drop tomorrow."

"More like a closetful of them," Stevie said glumly.

The girls followed their mothers into the house and headed straight for Regina's room. They climbed into bed, turned out the light, and went to sleep. There wasn't anything more to say.

13

"REGINA?"

At first it was a whisper, then louder.

"Regina."

There was a knock.

"Regina, are you awake?"

"Girls—you need to wake up."

"Regina, Stevie. You have to get up. There are some people here to see you."

That sounded serious. Stevie sat up and looked around her. She was in a strange bedroom. No, she knew it. She'd been there before. She was in Regina's bedroom. That was Regina's mother talking. There was something very bright nearby. It was the sun coming through the window.

That didn't seem possible, though. She'd only just gone to sleep.

"Get washed and dressed right away," said Mrs. Evans. "Something has happened. They need your help."

Once the girls assured her that they were more or less awake and understood her message, Mrs. Evans left. The girls were now fully awake and the events of the previous evening were beginning to come back to Stevie. Those last two sentences Regina's mother had spoken couldn't possibly be good news.

The look on Regina's face made it clear that she'd had the same thought. The look had a name: dread.

Reluctantly the girls got up, washed, and pulled on some clothes. Stevie paused in front of the mirror. Her reflection showed the same face she'd always known, admittedly not usually with such big circles under the eyes, but familiar nonetheless. She was wearing a long-sleeved T-shirt and jeans—her favorite ones with the red embroidered design at the ankles— and a rather ratty pair of sneakers. It might not be very stylish, but she thought the look reflected her personality. She wondered how she would feel about horizontal stripes—or would she be in one of those places that made you wear orange? Orange wasn't a good color for her. Lisa had told her that when she'd worn an orange T-shirt one day. Would Lisa and Carole be able to visit her? Would she ever see them again? She sighed and turned out the light. Time to face the music.

Stevie and Regina descended the stairs to the second floor. Both their mothers were in the living room. It was eight-thirty in the morning. Stevie knew her mother was supposed to be at her appointment at nine o'clock.

"Don't you have to leave, Mom?" Stevie asked.

"I think this is more important," she answered. "I've already called the office and told them I'll be late."

"Oh," said Stevie.

Two men stood up as the girls walked into the room. Mrs. Evans introduced them. "Girls, these are Detectives Eaken and Martin. Detectives, this is my daughter, Regina Evans, and her friend, Stephanie Lake."

"Stevie," Stevie said, offering her hand politely just the way her mother had taught her and hoping that the men wouldn't put cuffs on her right away.

"Glad to meet you girls. I guess you're pretty tired,"

said Detective Martin. He was a middle-aged man with a narrow mustache that made him look like Walt Disney. *Maybe there's hope*, Stevie thought.

"Uh, yes," said Regina.

"Well, we know the whole neighborhood was up watching the excitement at the house on the corner," said Detective Eaken. He was younger than Detective Martin. He was a thin man with thin lips and creases at the edges of his eyes that Stevie thought were from looking very closely at everything. He didn't look like Walt Disney at all. And he didn't look very friendly, either. "I guess the whole neighborhood pretty much lost a night's sleep."

"Pretty much," Stevie agreed. She and Regina sat down. Mrs. Evans poured some coffee for the detectives and handed each of the girls a glass of orange juice.

"Well, it was a big night for us, too," said Detective Martin. "We've been combing through clues for hours. We were there last night, too, you know."

Stevie didn't recognize him, but she nodded anyway. It seemed the polite thing to do. The detective paused.

The mothers didn't move. They were waiting just

like their daughters. Stevie glanced over at her mother. Even in her hastily assembled outfit, Mrs. Lake managed to look like a lawyer. Her face was all business. Mrs. Evans, on the other hand, looked like a social worker, compassionate and interested. The mothers' appearances were wasted, however. It was clear to Stevie that the detectives were interested in only two people in the room—Stevie and Regina.

"I guess you have been busy," Stevie said, encouraging the man. "You guys took a lot of stuff out of there."

As soon as she said the words, she cringed, realizing that they *had* taken a lot of stuff out of there, some of which she and Regina wished they hadn't. Stevie found herself wishing that the floor would open below her, just as it had the night before, and swallow her up once again. Almost anything would be better than waiting for the detectives to get to the point.

"Yes, we did," said Detective Eaken. "And some of it was very interesting indeed. It all had to do with that house—you know, the one on the corner?"

"Yes, that one," said Mrs. Evans. "They've been ren-

131

ovating it for a long time. I guess the Perseys must be excited about moving in soon."

"Not real soon, ma'am," said Detective Martin. "I don't think they'd be too pleased with what's been going on in there."

Kids, break-ins, broken floors, fires. No, Stevie didn't think the Perseys would be too happy about any of that, either.

"Well, there was some funny business last night, I'll tell you," said Detective Martin.

"What happened?" Stevie's mother asked.

"That's what we'd like to know," said Detective Eaken. "It all started about midnight—a little before, actually."

Stevie sank back into the sofa. She knew she didn't want to hear any of this. Regina did the same thing.

Detective Martin pulled a little notebook out of his pocket and flipped some pages. Then he began talking.

"There was a mounted policeman on the street at that time," he said. "He was passing by that house— you know, the one on the corner where all the construction work is happening?" *Yes,* Stevie thought, *we all know which house.*

132

"Seems he thought he heard someone calling for help. He stayed there quite a while, trying to figure out where the sound was coming from. Funny guy, that officer. He's made a bunch of reports that didn't amount to anything, so people don't tend to take him very seriously. Officer who cried wolf, you know what I mean?" The man paused.

It took every single ounce of self-restraint that Stevie had not to look at Regina at that point. It was made easier by the fact that her mother looked at her. As soon as the man mentioned a horse, her mother seemed suspicious. Stevie didn't have to pretend she was interested in what the detective was saying. She *was* interested.

"Anyway, the guy couldn't figure it out, but he thought it was worth investigating. So he rode on to where he was meeting his partner and the two of them came back. The partner swears they stood there for fifteen minutes to listen together. They didn't hear anything."

Stevie knew it wouldn't be wise to tell the detective that the two horses hadn't waited at all. She clamped her lips together.

"But they filed a report anyway."

Stevie gulped some orange juice.

133

The detective continued. "Well, that brought out some guys in a squad car and a foot patrol. Naturally, the idea of someone calling for help, even if they couldn't be heard anymore, is not something that can be ignored by the New York Police Department."

"Naturally," said Mrs. Lake. Mrs. Evans agreed. The girls nodded.

"So, they investigated. The squad car guys didn't find anything at first, but they went into the alley next to the building on the other side of the block. You know the place?"

Regina nodded.

"Sure," said her mother.

"Well, they were looking around the yards for anything suspicious, and they saw something. They reported . . ." He flipped some more pages in his notebook. "They saw a large number of people, perhaps half a dozen, says here, all at the back of that house at exactly 2:34 A.M. You know the house? The one that's being renovated?"

They nodded again, wondering why he kept trying to describe the house that they all knew. Stevie thought it was for dramatic effect. If that was the case, or even if it wasn't, it was working.

"What were those people doing?" Stevie's mother asked.

Stevie groaned. Lawyers seemed to know how to get to the heart of the matter, which was exactly where Stevie didn't want this to go.

"Well, that's what we'd like to know," said the detective. "The perps dispersed extremely quickly, like they all had a plan of where to go when they split up. They were in a big hurry, says here," he said, once again consulting his notebook.

Of course they disappeared as fast as possible, Stevie thought. They were tired and scared. They wanted to get home! She didn't share this thought with the detectives. Regina sat silent.

"Anyway, we think we've got them—or most of them," said Detective Eaken.

Stevie gulped.

"They've denied there was anyone else there, but we know there was. That's one thing the officers are absolutely sure about. Five or six, they said in their reports. We've got two in custody. They could see the perps' mode of egress—they'd come out of the basement of that building, the one on the corner—but the officers couldn't get over the fences as fast as those guys and they'd gone already, like I said."

Two. Which two? It must be Peter and Ann, Stevie thought. Her heart sank for her friends.

"Well, this escape action, plus the apparently unfounded cries for help, led to a full-scale investigation of the entire house, as you can imagine, ma'ams," said Detective Eaken. "Full-scale," he repeated.

"Of course!" Stevie's mother said.

"That's what we saw last night," said Mrs. Evans.

"Yes, ma'am," said Detective Martin. "And when they gained entrance into the building, what they found was very interesting. Very interesting, indeed."

And incriminating, Stevie thought, still trying to sink into the depths of the sofa.

"And incriminating," said Detective Martin.

At that moment Detective Eaken produced the very object that both Regina and Stevie had dreaded seeing. He reached into a large canvas bag and pulled out Regina's backpack. He put it on the coffee table.

Mrs. Evans's brow furrowed. Regina paled. Stevie did, too. Mrs. Lake just looked. Of course, she wouldn't have recognized it.

"There was nobody in the house," said Detective Eaken. "Nobody at all. They searched the place as much as they could, given the amount of construction going on."

"It must be almost done," said Mrs. Evans. "They've been working on it for over a year, and I know the Perseys are hoping to move in very soon."

"Not likely, ma'am," said Detective Martin. "Not for a long time."

"Why?" asked Mrs. Evans.

"Because the place is nowhere near ready. Almost no work has been done and there are dangers everywhere. In fact, there's even a big hole in the floor in what's supposed to be the kitchen. There are no stairs above the parlor floor."

"But the Perseys have paid him a fortune! Estelle told me herself!"

"Well, she may have paid a fortune, but it hasn't been used for her benefit. More likely, it's been used for the contractor's benefit and is probably safely tucked into a Swiss bank account by now."

"He keeps sending her receipts for all the work he's done," said Mrs. Evans.

"I think you could more correctly refer to that as the work he's *claimed* to have done," said Detective Martin.

"See, what we found there were dozens of files. In fact,

there was a whole room of filing cabinets and cartons that were filled with papers about work he'd been paid for at that house and at several other sites. This guy is a big-time fraud. I mean, big-time. Frank Justin is the man's name, and he's got a guy who works with him named Maurice Ayers. We'd thought there was some funny business going on for a while, since the buildings department found a pattern of problems with work he's done. We couldn't prove anything, though. We suspected bribery and extortion plus outright fraud, but there was no concrete evidence. Until last night."

Detective Martin continued the story. "What we found when we got into the house is enough evidence to send these guys up the river for a very long time. One interesting thing was that there was evidence of a fire, indicating the likelihood of some sort of insurance fraud scheme as well. These men are bad, big-time, and last night's investigation is the culmination of a major effort on our part. It seems ironic that the whole thing came together just because one mounted policeman thought he heard someone calling for help. Can you imagine that?"

Stevie could imagine that.

"Of course, since we've had them under investigation, we knew where to find them. They've both been apprehended and are in custody now."

Apprehended. That meant arrested. That meant that the two people they'd caught weren't Peter and Ann. It was Frank and Maurice. *So what about Peter and Ann?* Stevie thought.

"These guys were into a lot of things," said Detective Martin. "And last night's investigation suggests there's another side to this, too."

That was when he looked at the backpack and then at Regina.

"Do you recognize this backpack?" he asked.

Stevie could tell that Regina was wrestling with the truth. However, since the backpack had a large ID tag, and Regina's name and address were clearly written on it, there didn't seem to be much point in trying to deny it.

"Why, that's mine!" she said as if she'd just recognized it.

"We thought so," said Detective Martin. "This was found in the room where all the evidence was stored," he continued.

Stevie thought it best to say nothing and wait. Regina must've thought the same thing.

"It's a good thing that all he got was your backpack," said Detective Eaken. "That's one bad man, and if he wanted to get more, he'd find a way."

"Anyhow," said Detective Martin, "I'm sure you'll be glad to have that back. It had some food in it and some candles and flashlights, which our lab is going over, but it also contained some math homework, and the lab boys thought you'd be glad to have that back."

"Thank you," Regina squeaked.

"We thought you wouldn't want your math homework to get into the wrong hands," said Detective Martin.

And then he winked.

Stevie was sure of it. It was definitely a wink and it was definitely aimed at Regina and herself and not at either of the mothers. The detective *winked!*

The men stood up. "Thank you, ladies," he said to the mothers and girls. "We're awfully sorry to disturb your morning, but we wanted to return this stolen property to its rightful owner."

Stevie and Regina stood up, too—it was the polite thing to do—even though it was very hard because their knees were shaking.

"Um, we don't think we'll need any further involvement from the girls," said Detective Martin. "I'm sure we'll have enough evidence to convict those guys for fraud without going into the issue of backpack theft. We wouldn't want to subject these nice girls to any unnecessary court appearances."

"Of course not," said Mrs. Evans. She escorted the men downstairs to the front door and then returned to the living room.

Everyone sat down again. Nobody spoke for a few minutes.

Finally Mrs. Lake broke the silence. She pointed to the backpack.

"Stevie? Do you know anything about this?" she asked.

Regina nudged her. "The Fifth. Plead the Fifth!" she mumbled clearly enough for everybody to hear.

Stevie weighed her options very quickly and then shook her head.

"I never could fool my mom," she said to Regina. "She's a real truth machine and she always knows everything because she knows me so well. This time, what she knows, and I don't even have to tell her, is that somehow it was her daughter, her only daughter whom she loves very, *very* much, who provided the critical piece of the puzzle that enabled the police to round up an entire gang of crooked contractors. In the end she'll be proud of me. But right now she knows I need more sleep. A lot more sleep. Right, Mom?" she asked, and then looked hopefully at her mother.

Mrs. Lake shook her head. "I plead the Fifth," Stevie's mother said.

14

"YOU *WHAT?*" CAROLE asked.

"Helped the police catch a ring of crooked contractors," Stevie repeated.

"I don't get it," said Lisa.

The three of them were sitting on bales of hay at Pine Hollow. They didn't have long to talk because Stevie was technically grounded for a week, but her mother had allowed her to go to the stable to talk to Deborah, and she'd managed to arrange a meeting with her best friends as well. She'd shared every detail of her adventure—and her misadventure.

"It was part of one of the biggest contractor fraud

rings in the country," Stevie informed her friends. "See, Deborah thinks that this guy is connected to the people she's been investigating down here."

"Only Stevie," said Lisa.

"What?" Stevie asked.

"Only you would go to New York, break into someone else's property, set a fire, fall through a floor, and come out a hero."

Stevie nodded. "My thoughts exactly, but I can't take all the credit. Regina was there, too. I'll tell you one thing for sure, though, and that is that I'm *never* doing anything like that again. That was scary!"

"I bet Deborah was grateful for the inside scoop," said Carole.

"She was, but there were a few little details I left out when I was talking with her."

"Like the truth?" Carole asked.

"No, everything I told her was true," Stevie said. "I just didn't want to confuse her with unnecessary facts. I mean, there were some things that just don't need to appear in print anyplace my parents might possibly read them. I did tell her about the mounted policeman, though. She said Max was going to love that part, but she wasn't sure her readers would care much."

"Not care about the horse?" Carole asked, shocked.

Stevie laughed. It was just like Carole to focus on the horse and not the policeman or the cry for help. Lisa laughed, too.

"How did you feel about what you did—I mean the part you didn't tell Deborah about?" asked Lisa.

Stevie didn't have to think very hard to answer that. "Awful," she said. "It didn't seem so bad when we were just having some fun in what we thought was an abandoned building—or at least a forgotten one. But when we did things that damaged it—like accidentally starting the fire—I felt terrible. I can usually come up with some pretty good excuses when I get into trouble, but not this time. I mean, I'm not confessing or anything. But everybody knows what we did was wrong; otherwise why would my parents ground me for a week? All the other kids got punished one way or another, too, except Gordon. Nobody's telling on him. Even though the end has a silver lining, it was pretty stupid, wasn't it?"

That was a question Lisa and Carole didn't really think needed an answer.

"So how did it go with Maxi?" Stevie asked, happy to change the subject.

"It was tough at first," said Lisa. "Then Mrs. Reg

helped us discover the secret." She told Stevie the story about the stallion.

"Oh, of course," Stevie said. "She wanted to ride, didn't she?"

"Yes," Lisa said. "And as soon as we let her have her own way, she was happy, cheerful, and cooperative. In the last few days every time we've wanted her to do something or to stop doing something, we've bribed her with an offer of riding or threatened her with not riding."

"I wonder . . . ," said Stevie.

"What?" Carole asked.

"I wonder if we could get Mrs. Reg to tell that story to my parents so that they could understand the best way to get me to behave is to let me do exactly what I want to do."

"Go for it!" Lisa said, laughing.

"It's pointless," said Carole. "You always do exactly what you want to do anyway."

Stevie threw a handful of hay at Carole. But she didn't deny the truth of her friend's statement.

"Oh, one thing," said Carole.

"What?"

"Well, you told us you were looking for a bucket in the broom closet, and then you told Regina to come over and look at something. What was it?"

"Oh, that," said Stevie. "Yeah. You would have loved it."

"What?" Lisa asked.

Stevie smiled. "It was a whole stack of back issues of *Horsemanship*!"

Lisa smiled.

Carole didn't. She was too interested and excited to smile. "Did the police take them or do you think they're still there?" she asked.

Her friends laughed and hugged her. Stevie was very glad to be back home with people who loved and understood her.

ABOUT THE AUTHOR

BONNIE BRYANT is the author of more than a hundred books about horses, including The Saddle Club series, The Saddle Club Super Editions, the Pony Tails series, and Pine Hollow, which follows the Saddle Club girls into their teens. She has also written novels and movie novelizations under her married name, B. B. Hiller.

Ms. Bryant began writing The Saddle Club in 1986. Although she had done some riding before that, she intensified her studies then and found herself learning right along with her characters Stevie, Carole, and Lisa. She claims that they are all much better riders than she is.

Ms. Bryant was born and raised in New York City. She still lives there, in Greenwich Village, with her two sons.

Don't miss the next exciting
Saddle Club adventure . . .

HORSE FEATHERS
Saddle Club #98

Stevie Lake entered a contest to win a down com-
forter. Instead she got a new "family"—a nestful of
goose eggs. When the eggs hatch, it's love at first
sight for Stevie and the goslings. Now Stevie is
learning that being a mom is hard work—the
goslings want to go everywhere she goes, even to
Pine Hollow. Stevie has to keep her "kids" safe
while she tries to learn a new skill—vaulting.

The Saddle Club is determined to master vaulting and show Veronica diAngelo that success takes
more than fancy coaches. Can they pull this off?
Or is The Saddle Club plus eight goslings and one
vaulting horse a recipe for disaster?

MEET
the SADDLE CLUB

Horse lover CAROLE . . .
Practical joker STEVIE . . .
Straight-A LISA . . .

THE SADDLE CLUB SUPER EDITIONS

THE SADDLE CLUB SPECIAL EDITIONS

PINE HOLLOW

by Bonnie Bryant

*B*est friends Stevie, Carole, and Lisa have always stuck together. But everything has changed now that they're in high school. They've got boyfriends, jobs, and serious questions that they must grapple with on their own.

More and more they're discovering that sometimes even the best of friends can't solve your most serious problems.

Does this change in their lives mark the end of everything, or a brand-new beginning?

BFYR 240

Bantam